Blessing

Birds

By Janetta Fudge-Messmer

Lisa:

Kindness is the answer!

Blessings!
Janetta Fudge Messmer

DEDICATION

I don't know Chris Rosati, but he inspired the theme of this novel. I '**met**' Chris while watching a story Steve Hartman did on the CBS Evening News. Chris, a man dying of ALS, told Steve he wanted to commandeer a Krispy Kreme truck and give away the donuts to make people smile.

Over the next two years, Steve Hartman did follow-up stories on Chris and told about more of his Random Acts of Kindness. The last interview Steve did on Chris Rosati announced his death at age 46. I cried, but in my heart I knew I'd witnessed an example of a life well lived.

Thank you, Chris Rosati. Kindness can change the world. To read more of his story, go to: www.cbsnews.com/news/chris-rosati

CHAPTER ONE

"She's up to something, Mary and we're going to find out what it is." Betsy peeked out of the laundry room window at the taillights on an Uber sedan.

The very one carrying their friend, Rose. And the one exiting the campground to who knew where for the second time in a week.

"I agree it's a tad strange since we're leaving in two days." Mary folded a towel and put it in her basket.

"Ah huh."

"But since Larry drove the men to church today in their car, maybe she needed to run an errand for Sassy Seconds *Two* and didn't want to ask you to borrow your truck."

"Sounds plausible, but Rosie always includes us in her adventures. I ask, why didn't she today or on Monday, when she drove her own car? About borrowing our truck, if she needed to go somewhere, she knows where my keys are." Betsy picked up her basket of clothes.

"It is a mystery. And—"

"One we're going to solve. If it's the last thing I

do." Betsy walked to the door and pushed it open. "Mary, she has mischief written all over her face." Bets chuckled. "and nowhere does it say she's hired a car to pick her up to get her hair done. 'Cause she needs a trim."

"I'm going to tell her what you said about her unkempt doo."

"Good, and I hope it riles her up enough to tell us what she's doing."

"I doubt it."

"Whatever it is, we're going to find out what Mrs. Sneaky Pants is up to. Let's put our laundry away and meet back at the picnic table to discuss our next step."

Bets didn't wait for Mary's "yay" or "nay", but hurried to her RV. While she put the clothes away, she prayed the Lord kept Rosie out of trouble. "Amen."

"Knock. Knock."

"I'm almost there." Betsy grabbed a pen and notepad off her desk, but her eyes traveled to her open laptop. "Yes, after I get done figuring out what Rosie's doing, I'll come back in and write, write, write. Matilda, I'll take you for a walk too."

"Betsy, do you want me to come in there?"

"No, I'm on my way." Betsy hurried down the stairs and took her place at the picnic table. Pen and paper in hand. "Sorry for the delay, but my computer and pooch were vying for my attention. I informed them I was figuring out another pressing matter."

"This deal with Rose has me baffled too."

"It's past me being baffled. I tease her about being off her meds, but this time I'm wondering if the devil hasn't set up shop inside her chubby body." Betsy put her hand over her mouth. "I didn't just say that? Did I?"

"Which part?" Mary laughed. "And, no, evil has not gripped our friend. I do suggest we talk to Larry and see if he can shed light on his wife's odder-than-normal behavior."

"Good idea, but I'd rather solve it ourselves. If I know Larry, he hasn't noticed anything different about Rosie. When the men are finishing up a job, all three of us ladies could parade around in a cellophane nightgown and they'd ask us, "what's for dinner?"

"Bets, I hope if we did this we're inside one of our RVs. Wouldn't want the campground to call the police on three crazy, and almost naked, women."

"How about we keep our clothes on and get down to business. I suggest the next time we see Rosie taking off, we follow her."

"Betsy, did you hear what you said? We're going to do surveillance in a honking dually truck?" Mary stopped and slapped the table. "I'll bet she'll never see us. Oh, but what about the noise a diesel truck makes?"

"You've made your point. What's your suggestion, Miss Logical One?"

"Let's play her game. Hire our own Uber and have them tail her to where she's going."

"Good idea, but there's a slight problem with your arrangement." Betsy watched Mary to see if she'd figured it out. When she didn't appear to see the problem, Bets continued, "Dear, we don't know when Rose is leaving again. We have to have the driver here, so we can follow her."

"Guess I now know why I didn't go into detective work."

"And I guess our only solution is to ask Rosie what she's up to." Betsy had another thought. "I know what we can do. We'll borrow my next door neighbor's car. She told me, after we got back from Colorado, her car was available anytime to take it to the beach."

"I'd say our investigative work has begun."

"Tomorrow, my friend. Today my backside is in the chair to put my book proposal together."

"See you then."

~~~

The next morning Betsy's phone beeped. She expected to see Rose or Mary's face and their number, but instead Larry's appeared. "Hello."

"Bets, is my wife over there?"

"No, haven't seen her. Why?"

"This is too much info, but I left to take a shower and when I got back, she's gone and so is our car."

Shooty poop. We missed her.

"This oddity goes along with yesterday, Betsy. On our way home from helping at church, we stopped at Sassy Seconds *Two.* I expected to see Rosie, but Everly said she hadn't seen her in days. Now I have a charge on our credit card for Uber. What is an Uber?"

Betsy wanted to laugh, but decided her friend didn't need hilarity at the moment. "Lar, it's like a taxi service."

"What? Why'd she need—"

"Mary and I are wondering the same thing. And since she's left again, our plan will have to wait for the next time she goes somewhere."

"Plan? For what?"

Betsy heard a sigh on the other end of the line and imagined Larry pacing the floor of their Class C. As she did in their 5th wheel. Ben stared at her from the table, but kept eating his cereal.

"Larry, we're concerned about Rosie and we were going to follow her to wherever she ended up. It's not like her not to take Mary and me along. I'm counting on that it's not illegal, but it's weird even for your wife to take off and not tell anyone."

"Well, I have a plan of my own and when Ben, Jeff and I finish at church today, we'll come home and Rosebud will have some explaining to do."

"Can we come over and watch?"

"Pull up a chair. Knowing Rose, she'll earn a Best Actress award for her acting ability, telling us about it. Or I should say, how to get herself out of the mess she put herself, and others, into."

Betsy laughed and Larry joined in. Their merriment lasted until Ben stood up and stared at her. "Larry, I need to go. If I see your wife before you get home, mums the word. I want to see the show you have planned."

"Tell Ben I'm ready to go whenever he is."

"I will. Enjoy your day."

Betsy lay her phone on the counter and turned to her hubby. "Larry's waiting on you."

"I heard."

"And he'll tell you what we talked about. As Mary said, "It's a mystery." And I have to agree."

"When you're dealing with Rosie, that's an understatement." Ben leaned down to kiss her, but stopped and said, "Hon, why are you looking at me like my head's on backwards? I heard most of your conversation with Larry."

"Then you'll understand when I tell you I'll have the chairs set up for everyone when you get home from work today."

"Put our seats front and center. This'll be good. Why don't you and Mary make popcorn? It's show time."

"It is, Ben." Larry opened the screen and peered in. "And if we don't get to church and finish our job there, we'll miss it."

Betsy scooted Ben to the door and on his way down the stairs, he fired back, "Don't forget the popcorn. We'll be home around 4:30."

CHAPTER TWO

"Larry, we can speculate all day about Rose's comings and goings," Ben talked as they walked into the church. "But we'll have to wait and see."

"Those words don't give me comfort, Benjamin."

"But these will." Pastor Cheavers came out of his office. "I'm glad I caught you guys before you got to work on the last of the painting. Greg finished it this morning."

"What did he do, show up at the crack of dawn?"

"No, he didn't." Greg stepped out of the door to one of the offices. "I wanted to make sure it was done right."

"Gotta love a man with his wits about him so early in the morning."

"As I was saying," the pastor cleared his throat. "We've got a job of setting sod at a community center today. It's six or seven pallets. Get it done and I can send you gentleman off to help other souls."

Jeff moved forward. "We'd be on the road again in less time if the fifth person, you, came along and helped."

"I'll take you up on the offer, and buy lunch too. Let me check my calendar."

"Your calendar is completely clear, sir." The woman's words, and then laughter, burst forth from the office Greg stepped out of earlier.

"Thanks, Kay." The pastor smiled then added, "The help you get these days."

"She's a keeper, and she'll have water and two aspirin ready when you return later today."

Kay's remarks reminded Ben of his wife and the other two women. Their sense of humor kept him and the other men on their toes at all times. And later in the afternoon, Rosie's tales would entertain them. *Can't wait to see how she explains her absences.*

"Are we ready to go to work?" Larry tapped his foot. "Daylight's a wasting."

"It's nine o'clock in the morning."

"Jeff, we need to get moving. There's popcorn and a performance when we get home tonight."

"Does this production have to do with Rose? Mary mentioned she'd been acting more peculiar than normal. Is that even possible?"

"Yes, and I suggest we get going." Larry opened the side door and gestured for the men to follow him.

"Are one of you going to fill us in on what you were talking about a minute ago? Sounded like someone is in the need of prayer."

"Pastor Cheavers, prayers are appreciated. Since you've met Rosie, you'll understand my next statement. She's acting odd, even by her standards. Tonight we'll find out what's going on with her. You two can come over if you want to."

"Have someone record it since we're taping a

webinar tonight."

"You don't know what you're missing."

"I don't, Ben, but Larry, you need to turn at the next corner. You'll go two miles and the community center is on the right."

All the while Larry drove, he filled Greg and the pastor in on Rose's strange behavior. "To top it off, she rented an Uber. I've never heard of such a thing. Don't know what she's doing, but I'm excited for this day to end so we can find out."

After Larry pulled into the parking lot, Ben spied the pallets next to where his friend parked. It had been years since he'd laid sod, and without laying any, his back yelled at him to get the pain reliever out of Larry's console.

He took two and offered them to the others. "Any takers."

"Not me. I'm in shape with all the bike riding we've been doing."

"Lar, you won't be using the same muscles." Jeff opened the front door and jumped out.

"Keep your back straight and lift with your legs." Pastor Cheavers laughed. "Kay gave one of the helpers those instructions the other day when he was lifting a heavy box."

"She's a bevy of information."

"That she is, Ben. How about we get busy, so you three can get home?"

"I vote we take our time. The more I think about it – I *don't* want to find out what my wife is up to."

"I do," Ben and Jeff said the two-word sentence and all the men laughed.

For the rest of the morning, they rolled out the sod

on the front and side yard of the community center. On occasion, volunteers brought them water. Ben heard Jeff tell the young man, "leave a half dozen this time. I feel there's a bath in my future."

"Jeff, we baptized you in Boulder at the job site. Remember? No need to douse yourself again."

"The only thing I recollect about Boulder, Mr. Wilford, is Ben yelling at one of the helpers."

"Don't remind me. Not one of my better days."

"If memory serves me right, it worked out fine. I do wish one of us had stayed in touch with Christopher. I'd like to know what happened to him."

"Larry, working with all of you, I'm positive he's doing fine." The pastor dabbed at his forehead with his sleeve. "Hey, is anyone ready for lunch?"

"Don't say it, Ben. We're not eating at Taco Bell."

"I haven't eaten there in years. Let's go." Greg bounded to the car.

Ben opened the driver's door for Larry. "Are you coming? The man spoke. Taco Bell it is."

~~~

After the food arrived, Ben chowed down on his burrito. His phone chirped before he swallowed and he hoped the men understood when he said, "It's my wife." He read the text and since he'd taken a bite, he started to cough.

"If you live long enough, please tell us what's going on."

Ben took a drink and with a gravelly voice uttered, "Thanks for the concern for me almost dying over here."

"Your lips weren't turning blue. Now about the text. It has to be about my wife."

"It was. Betsy said Rosie returned home and is hiding out in your RV. Bets didn't know which direction she came in from, but her beet red face made her think the Uber driver dropped her off at the shopping center across the street."

"This afternoon can't get over soon enough." Larry grinned from ear to ear.

"Man, you're enjoying this way too much."

"Jeff, you have no idea how many times my wife has gotten my goat. Today it's my turn."

Ben finished his burrito and the others hurried through their meals, as well. All seemed to want to get Larry home sooner than later. Even though the pastor and Greg opted out of the evening's entertainment, he'd text them in the morning to let them know the outcome.

This cracked him up and after Ben's tablemates stared, he filled them in on what had transpired in his head then added. "All I can say, Pastor Cheavers and Greg, you two better pray like you've never prayed before. We'll need it."

"We will, and it's time to go. Sod is waiting."

Larry returned them to the community center and they made haste of emptying the rest of the pallets. At 3:10 Jeff unrolled the last one and a loud shout resonated through the volunteers and staff.

"I don't know what we'll do without you three, but wherever your RVs take you, you'll bless the people you come in contact with. Before that happens, don't forget to pick up the letter of recommendation from Kay."

They piled into Larry's car and when they reached the church, Ben told the others to wait and he'd go get the letter. On his way back, he noticed all the men stood outside the car, talking.

"Are we going to stand here all day, or are we going home? I'm famished."

"Me too." Jeff hugged the pastors, and then stepped back. "I don't know about my cohorts, but I've enjoyed working with you two the last four months. Count on us for next season. We'll be back in October or November."

"He'll have a list made out for things he wants done." Greg gave a half smile. "And while you're on the road, pray no hurricanes head our way, or you'll have even more work when you get back here."

"In any case, we'll have another pair of hands with us when we return to Florida in the fall. Peter Webster, my future nephew-in-law, will be along to help. My wife says we'll like him."

"Looking forward to meeting him. But first, you have another pressing matter. Larry's wife is home and you need to get going." Pastor Cheavers laughed then said, "We'll be praying for you."

"Please do."

CHAPTER THREE

"**5** mins. away. Popcorn & chairs. Grab Rose." Betsy read the text from Ben and called Mary. They met near the picnic table and set the stage. Then they retrieved the bowls of the asked-for snack and ventured outside again.

Betsy saw Larry's car drive in. Before they made too much racket, she strolled over and knocked on the Wilford's door to alert the unsuspecting 'star' her audience awaited her arrival.

The older woman opened her door and Betsy speculated if a person's eyes bulged any more, they'd pop out of their sockets and she'd have to pick them up off the ground and dust them off.

Her friend's breathing appeared abnormal as well. And when Betsy asked, "Rosie, can you come out here?" it didn't improve any.

"Yes, dear. Come on out." Larry walked over to his RV. "Don't be shy, Rosebud."

"What's going on? Why are our lawn chairs set up this way? Why do I smell popcorn? Are we watching a movie? Where's the TV?" Rose stepped out of her RV and turned in all different directions.

"No, we're not watching a movie, but we're about to witness quite the show." Larry grinned, but his expression showed little happiness as he seated himself in one of the lawn chairs.

"What are you talking about, old man? Is this about me turning your underwear pink last week. Don't see why you'd ask the Early Birds here to confront me about it. All I can say, sometimes you're not firing off all your pistons either." Rose snorted.

"Boxers, or their color, has nothing to do with why everyone's here. But the 'not always firing off all pistons' is exactly why we're sitting here. Rosie, what in the world is going on with you, and why have you started renting cars to pick you up?"

Again Rose's eyes wanted to do something other than stay in her head, but the transformation from a crazed person into an actor almost caused the palm trees above the Early Birds heads to lose their fronds.

"Oh, that little detail. I can explain every bit of it. I can do it in four words - Haphazardly Handing Out Hospitality. Or Helpfulness. I haven't decided which name I like better."

Larry leapt to his feet and headed in the direction of their RV, but must have changed his mind and stood in front of his wife. "Rosie, your four words, or whatever you just said explains nothing."

"Yes, it does. You've all heard of Random Acts of Kindness. I've made up a new name for the same thing. I suggest on our trip up the East Coast, we call what we're doing H.H.H. - Haphazardly—"

"Larry, can I take this one?" Betsy almost catapulted out of her chair as she spoke.

"Go for it. I'm happy to share."

"Rose, I love, love, love the name and the concept. However, it doesn't explain why you set out on this new venture. Alone. Usually, you want an audience to observe what it is you're doing."

"Which is my customary way of doing things, but this time I wanted to experiment. Do nice gestures on unsuspecting people before I brought it to the group. Obviously, I can't do anything without a crowd of people wanting to know my every move."

"Dear, we were concerned." Larry tried to smile, but from Betsy's angle, his face still refused to cooperate. Then he added, "Rose, I don't know if I'm buying your saintly servanthood. Tell us how you helped humanity. I know we're all waiting to hear it."

Again, in less than five minutes, Rosie's eyes darted from side to side as if she tried to find a good place to land them. But her extra-long pause, before she gave an answer, surprised Betsy. *Never known Rosie to be at a loss for words.*

The phenomenon playing out in front of them must have confounded Larry too. He took one of the chairs and pointed to it. "Rose, let me help you sit down. Looks like what you have to say will take a while."

"Or, all night, if she doesn't start soon." The noise Betsy expelled resembled her friend's.

Larry retook his seat and once again silence filled the air. He glanced in his wife's direction and reiterated, "Rosebud, if we have to, we will wait for your story until morning. Go ahead. We're all ears."

"Funny you'd ask for a story, because I have a whopper."

Betsy watched her best friend and from the

numerous blinks taking place, she decided Rosie still tried to keep her eyes where they belonged. No doubt when the narrative began, it'd be worth the time it took to tell it.

"I saw him, standing there on the street corner. Larry, I heard your voice in my head, 'Rosebud, what are you doing?', but I continued my trek. When I reached the sidewalk, I wanted to laugh. The man held his "Need money for food" sign to his chest as if he was protecting himself from me."

"Do you blame him?"

"Be quiet, Bets. She's on a roll." Jeff crossed his arms over his chest.

"As I was saying, I marched up to him and in my kindest voice said, "Sir, I'm only wanting to give you water and these food coupons." Rose extended her hand, as if she gave them out again. "I didn't say anything about the H.H.H ministry. Didn't want to scare him."

"H.H.H.?"

"Benjamin Stevenson, are you sleeping over there?"

"Hon, H.H.H. stands for Haphazardly Handing Out Hospitality."

"Or Helpfulness, Betsy. Anyway, the man took the coupons. After he peered at them, his uproarious laughter blanketed the area. It was as if I stood in the middle of a hyena's cage. He also waved them as if they were Old Glory."

"Why did the man have such a reaction to the gift you gave him?" Larry rested his arms on his chest too. "May I ask where you bought the coupons?"

"Hold on. It's coming down the pike." Rose's cheeks took on a brighter pinkish tint. "For some reason, the fellow started to stutter. After a length of time, he said, 'Ma'am, you do…know…about Cantaloupes, don't…you?'"

"I assured him I'd heard of Cantaloupes since it was where I'd bought the coupons. Then I added, "The young woman standing behind the counter seemed nice when I visited with her. Nothing appeared out of the ordinary. I think."

Betsy's chair tilted and almost tipped over. And it appeared the other Early Birds tried to get themselves under control too. If she had to gauge their level of laughter, it ranked up to the hysterics in Colorado Springs with their dogs, Matilda and Baby.

"I know why you're laughing, but I didn't have a clue when the man's reaction matched yours. I finally asked him, "Are you alright?"' His answer, 'I've never been better. They *do* sell food at Cantaloupes, but did you happen to see what the women wore when you got the coupons?'"

"What were they wearing, dear, when you visited them?" Larry wiped at his eyes.

"Let me finish. After he asked me the question, I pondered it for a minute. Then the lightbulb came on. No doubt my face touched on every shade of crimson in the color wheel God created."

"Sort of like what you're doing right now?" Betsy had to ask.

"Yeppers. And I told the man to hand them over and I'd be right back with ones better suited to the situation. So there you have it Early Birds. One H.H.H. completed, and more to follow. As I like to say, we're spreading small snippets of the Savior's love. Everywhere we go."

Betsy heard Rose's tale and concluded her friend stretched the truth farther than the distance between Florida and the Fiji Islands. But she'd keep it to herself. When Mary and she found time alone with Rosie, then she'd pounce on her to tell them the truth.

"I don't know if I believe you, dear, but helping out our fellow man any way we can is always a winner. Next time, though, check out where you're buying coupons first." Larry got up and kissed his wife on the cheek.

More laughter broke out and in the midst of their amusement, Ben suggested, "I don't know about any of you, but I'm hungry. Do you want to go with me to my favorite Mexican place?"

"No. Already been there once today. I think Rose and I will eat in tonight. Come on, dear, we have lots to talk about."

CHAPTER FOUR

"Betsy, you've said it before, but tonight I'm using it. I'd love to be a mouse right now at the Wilford's," Ben said as he stirred the chicken noodle soup.

"Why's that?"

"Either she has Larry, and all of us buffaloed, or she's come up with the plan of the century. Her theatrics included at no charge." Ben laughed so hard tears slid down his cheeks and Matilda came out from under the table and looked up at him.

"Mats, your dad's having a fit and if he doesn't quiet down, the manager is going to come visit."

Ben walked over, still chuckling and opened the pantry. "What did we do with her 'Me Cute' shirt?"

"Stuck it in a drawer in the bedroom. I thought of the exact same thing when we were cracking up outside. Think we beat the prank in Colorado by a mile tonight. I've never heard such a tall tale."

"Tall tale. You think—"

"I think you need to turn the soup down. Then you can hand me the crackers and butter. Remember, you're hungry."

Ben filled the bowls and brought the soup over to the table. Matilda followed him, so he got her bowl and filled it with her dog food. "Mats, do you want a little tasty broth in your dinner too?" He took his spoon and blew on it, pouring it on the morsels.

"Benjamin, I'm surprised you don't invite our pooch to join us at the table."

"Can we?" Ben patted his leg and Matilda put her front paws on him.

"No, it'd take too long to train her to use the utensils."

"You're no fun."

"Ah huh."

Ben took a bite of the piping hot soup and watched Betsy. The outdoors held her interest. Not her dinner. Her spoon stayed next to her dish. Every so often she'd reach for a cracker, but change her mind and return to staring out the window.

"I'm no psychiatrist, but I sense something's bothering you. Want to elaborate?"

"It's not you, dear, for a change. Not that I'm a nag." Betsy picked up her spoon then sat it down again. "I don't know about you, but Rosie's story seems way too farfetched. Even for her."

"It does, but for right now I'm going to believe her. If she's pulling our chains, I'll tell her I enjoyed her story. Now eat. You need your strength." Ben buttered a cracker and stuck it in his mouth.

"Why do I need my strength?"

"For when Mary and you follow Rose to see what she's doing."

"You know me too well." Betsy laughed. "One things for sure, I hope it's tomorrow. Get this mystery over with. I'm an author, not a sleuth."

"How about we go over to the loveseat and—"

"You go ahead; I'm going to the bedroom."

"Leave Rosie alone. Anyway, the Wilford's have gone to bed."

"Not worrying about her anymore tonight. I have lots of work to do. My goal is to get my book proposal sent out before we leave." Betsy grabbed her laptop and headed upstairs. *Not that anything will happen with the book, if I do send it out.*

"I'll miss you." Ben flipped on the TV and Matilda came and joined him on the loveseat. "If you need a listening ear, let me know. There's never anything on TV."

"Will do."

~~~

For the next two hours Betsy put away her concerns for Rose and typed away on her proposal. One glaring problem persisted with finishing it—NO TITLE. Betsy, Ben, and their friends had racked their brain ever since she'd written The End. They'd come up empty.

"I've got it. Name it Heavenly Helpers." Ben suggested the title the day she returned from Colorado.

Betsy chuckled when the memory came to mind, and in all honesty, she'd loved his idea. And kept it on her short list. "Lord, finding the perfect title won't bring world peace. However, my book will look funny without one. Just saying. Help. AMEN!"

"Are you talking to your computer again?" Ben opened the door.

"No, I'm pleading with the man upstairs to intervene in naming my book. It's obvious all of us stink at coming up with a title. I forgot to tell you

Rose's idea from last week. Are you ready for it? She wanted me to call my novel: Crazy Birds On the Road...Again."

"It's true, but not a keeper. I still like the title I suggested."

"I do too. Maybe I'll type it in my proposal and see what the publisher thinks. Never know."

"I have another great idea. How about we go to bed? It's been a long day."

"Longer for some than others." Betsy chuckled as she picked up her laptop and put it on the dresser. She then pulled back the covers and snuggled in next to Ben and Matilda. "It's your turn to pray."

CHAPTER FIVE

Betsy woke up to a chirping sound, coming from her side table. Her eyes barely focused on the words Mary texted, "RW is on the move. Laundry room now."

A cannon couldn't have shot Bets out of bed faster, or dressed her quicker. Mary and she made it to the cement-block building in less than three minutes. Rose glanced at them when they rushed in, but continued taking clothes out of the dryer and folding them.

"When did you start getting up at this ungodly hour to do laundry?"

"A similar question lingers on my lips too, Bets. When did me doing laundry become a social event?" Rose rolled a t-shirt and placed it in her basket. "And, one might ask, 'Why are you here since you forgot an important item—your own dirty laundry?'"

Rose's quirky smile informed Betsy her friend enjoyed this early-morning encounter way too much. It also became clear either Mary or she better explain why they'd shown up. When Bets studied her friend, who had texted her, she only received a shrug.

Betsy waltzed over to the dryers. "Rosie, it's funny

you bring up 'dirty laundry'. I, oh, I mean Mary and I, have been wanting to ask you about..." Betsy let the sentence dangle, hoping Mary would jump in. She didn't. *Lord, I'm going in. Send me a life preserver.*

"Ask me what, Betsy? Mary?"

"How about we go back to last night. I loved your idea and the story of how you helped the gentleman—"

The door flung open and three men strolled into the laundry room. Each carried an overflowing basket of laundry. On their way to get to the end washers, each said, "Excuse me, ladies."

"You're fine. Now, what were you saying, Bets?"

"Let's let the men finish what they're doing. They don't want to hear women discussing the best way to remove a grease spot."

"I'd love to know your trick. My wife can't get a stain out to save her soul. It's why I'm doing it today. Anyway, we'll be out of your way in no time, and then you can talk all you want."

As promised, they completed their task and Betsy watched them walk over to the table across from the washers and sit down. If they listened, they'd hear what Betsy said, but she didn't care. The time had come to bring home the bacon. *Where did that come from?*

Betsy ignored the absurd phrase and plowed ahead. "Rosie, as I said, I love the idea of you helping the man, *however*, I'm not believing a word of it. No one gives a person down on their luck coupons to a girly joint.

"Fess up or Mary and I will follow you to find out what 'dirty laundry' you're hiding from all of us. Mrs. Wilford, your time is not your own from this minute forward."

While Betsy gave her friend a piece of her mind,

Rosie's expression resembled a wide-eyed deer about to meet his Lord and Savior on the highway of life. And the item Rose folded somehow took flight, landing behind the dryer she'd taken it out of.

"Oh Lord, don't let it be a pair of my undies."

Betsy heard Rose's whispered plea, and before anyone checked to see what landed back behind the dryer, one of the men yelled from the table, "Bruce, toss me one of the metal hangers over there."

The man caught it in mid-air and took the hanger apart. In no time, he'd leaned over the dryer and retrieved the item. When he brought it up for all to see – a pair of bright yellow underwear hung on the end of his makeshift grabber.

"I assume these are yours." The man dropped them on the dryer and rejoined his circle of friends. He turned and held out the hanger. "If you need this again. It'll be over here."

"Thank you, sir, I won't be needing it."

Bets eyeballed Rose, and her friend's face resembled the same one she wore the day she bit into the taco with extra-hot sauce. A wide range of wisecracks danced on Betsy's tongue, but she kept them under wrap.

Mary didn't stay silent. "See Rosie, your Haphazardly Handing Out Hospitality works both ways and it comes in all shapes and sizes."

"If you know what's good for you, you'll nip it, Mary. And if I hear you told the guys this story, I'll sneak into your RV and steal all your cute undies and hang them up for all the world to see."

"Rose, I believe you've lost your sense of humor. Hey, Mary, maybe we need to go check behind the washers and dryers. Might be where she left it – cozied right up next to her colorful underwear."

"Oh Ha! Ha!" Rose refolded the colorful undergarment and picked up her basket. "If you're interested, my car leaves in a half hour. With or without you." She opened the door and walked out. "Do not tell your hubbies what you're doing. If you do, you'll ride in the trunk."

~~~

Betsy hurried to her RV to change and, as always, their pooch met her at the door. "Matilda, where's your dad?" No answer came from her furry friend, but she saw a piece of paper on the counter.

"Lar forgot a couple of his tools at church. I know you won't miss me, you're too busy worrying about Rose. ☺"

She smiled at her hubby's note. And, yes, Rosie's recent behavior concerned her, but they'd find out soon enough what she'd gotten herself into. Betsy put on a different shirt and combed her hair then made her way to the Wilford's RV.

Mary walked through the grass to meet her. "Bets, where do you think she's taking us?"

"I have no idea, but if Ben hadn't taken the truck, I'd go grab the hard hats…just in case. Whatever it is, it'll have our friend's signature all over it. With neon lights flashing." Betsy laughed.

"Baby, you behave yourself. Mama will be awhile. Not sure where your dad is."

"Ben's note said they ran to church."

"Good to know." Rose locked her RV, and as she approached her car she stopped. "Ladies, you can laugh all you want. You can imagine all kinds of things I'm doing. You can even…oh, I can't think of anything else. Get in the car."

As with other trips they'd ventured out on together, giggles followed close behind them. But today Rosie's ability to drive seemed to become more treacherous with the extra supply of snickers going on.

And her next statement, as Rose drove down Summerlin, sealed the deal, "You two have to put these on." Rose tossed each of them a pillowcase she'd taken from under her front seat.

"I am not wearing this." Betsy held hers up.

"Me neither."

"Remember, I'm the keeper of the knowledge. You're not. Put them on, or I'm turning around."

"Mary, I'm glad I chose the back seat. I can duck down and no one can see me."

"I'll switch. Pull over, Rose."

"I'm doing no such thing. Put 'em on."

Betsy watched Mary put her flowered pillowcase on then she scrunched as far down in the front seat as humanly possible for a tall person. Bets donned hers and leaned over on the seat. The thought came to her, why did she bother with her hair before she left?

More laughter from the front seat ensued as Rose continued to drive. Betsy found no humor in any of this and said, "This is not funny. Pull this puppy over. I just found out I'm claustrophobic."

"No you're not, and there's no need to yell so loud. We're almost at our destination. I forgot to mention, when we get there, you have to stay in the car like you are. I have to set the stage."

"I'm going to set something when we stop, but it has little to do with the theatre. There is one good thing, if I ever have a kidnapped person in one of my books, I'll know exactly how they feel."

"I'll give you my take on it too, Bets."

"I'd appreciate it." Betsy fidgeted and found the other seat belt dug into her side. *This better get done soon, or I'm—*

"We're here. Now stay put until I tell you to come."

"Mary, I don't know about you, but I know how Matilda and Baby feel. Come. Are you going to put a leash on us too?"

"I won't be long. Stay."

"Another dog reference. Betsy, we're in trouble."

Bets heard a door slam and couldn't contain her laughter any longer. "I'm a writer, but I can never envision what Rose is going to do next. It's a surprise every minute with her."

"Every second. And, do I need to remind you we're talking to each other covered in a pillowcase?"

"This is why I write boo—" Betsy stopped when she heard a horn beeping. It stopped then tooted a dozen more times. "Mary, do you think that's our signal?"

"I don't know, but let's take a look."

Betsy ripped the case off her head and stared at a Class C motorhome with Rose as its driver. She waved a piece of paper, and her head stuck out the driver's side window. Both Mary and she opened their doors and got out.

"Mary. Betsy. Come over here. You can come too, Aaron," Rose hollered and flapped her arms like a chicken getting shot at.

They rushed over to the RV and Rose showed them what she held in her hand. "It's official. I can drive our mini monster anytime I want. I have a certificate, which makes me cer-ti-fied."

"Cer-ti-fi-able, maybe. Wow, Rosie, this is quite a surprise." Betsy held the certificate and true to her friend's word, it read: *Rose Wilford passed the Precision Brothers Driving Academy. Congratulations!!!*

"Want to take a ride?"

"Why not, but before we go I'm going back to the car to get my pillowcase. Mary, do you want yours?"

"Ladies, you won't need to cover your heads. Rose has passed our stringent requirements."

"And there were plenty of them. It's the Lord who saw me through each and every one of them." Rosie beamed.

"She is ready to hit the road."

"Perfect timing 'cause we're getting *on the road again,* bright and early tomorrow morning. Only this time, I'm driving. Jump in, girls, and I'll take you for a spin around the course."

CHAPTER SIX

"I don't know what our wives were doing over at the laundry room, but before we left I snuck over and looked in the window. A man stood waving a pair of underwear on the end of what looked like a hanger. Rosie didn't look too happy." Ben took a sip of coffee.

"When it involves my Rosie, and the other two ladies, nothing should shock any of us."

"Hope while we're gone that they get to the bottom of what's going on with Rose."

"I don't have a doubt they'll figure it out. By the way, I loved Rose's story last night. Mary and I talked about it and our vote goes to us doing Random Acts of Kindness, or the other name she called it."

"So, do you believe Rose's story?" Larry stabbed a piece of sausage and put it in his mouth.

"Not a word of it, but the concept has Mary and me ready to jump in our RV and get busy."

"Jeff, is your short-term memory going?" Larry slathered jelly on a piece of toast. "We're leaving in the morning, but if we don't get done eating, we'll still be putting things away at midnight."

"My mama taught me that you're not supposed to eat too quick. It'll clog your arteries faster."

"It's not the speed you eat it, Jeffrey, it's the food you eat." Larry popped another piece of sausage into his mouth.

"I'm telling Rose you're eating pure cholesterol again."

"She's so preoccupied, Ben, I could kick the bucket and she'd put me in the underneath compartment and keep on going."

Ben regretted taking a drink of coffee right when Larry lay that zinger on the table. Java squirted out of his nose and down the front of his beige t-shirt, which amused his tablemates even more.

Patrons at the popular restaurant stared at them when their amusement hit a fever's pitch. "Guys, we better keep it down. Shush." Ben finished cleaning up and grabbed the bill. "It's my treat since I was the morning's entertainment."

"Thanks. That'll help our budgets." Jeff put his wallet away.

"Not mine." Ben took out his keys. "Are you ready to go to church?"

~~~

Ben and Jeff waited in the truck while Larry picked up his forgotten items. And since they'd said their goodbyes yesterday, they didn't need to do it again. Or so Ben thought. In his rear-view mirror, three men came to the side of his truck.

"Thought you'd roll in here and not come in and tell us what happened last night. We're dying." Greg tapped on Ben's arm.

"Are you sure no one took a video?" The pastor

questioned. "I hear they're always looking for short films for the Academy Awards. Might have missed out on winning one of the statues."

"When it started, I didn't think to take out my phone. Our friend here, his wife kept us enthralled for a good twenty minutes." Ben glanced at Larry. "Since we're heading towards New York City, Lar, drop her at one of the theatres. They'd love to meet her."

"Dropping her somewhere is an option."

"You'd miss her."

"I would, Ben, for about—"

"All kidding aside, the small portion Larry told us does sound interesting. If we'd use the concept as a church, we'd have to double check what coupons we gave out." The pastor chuckled, along with Greg. Ben and the others hitched onto their party too.

When Larry pulled himself together, he said, "I want to believe her tale of helping humanity, but I'll wait to see if we do anymore. If it's forgotten, we'll find a church in the area we're in and help them."

"Whatever you do, the Lord loves a cheerful giver."

"I'm not up on the Bible like Ben and Larry, but I think that verse is talking about money. You know, tithing?"

"From the look on the pastor's face, we're going to have a church service out here on this parking lot." Greg pulled out his phone, and soon held it out for the preacher to take it. "I googled the verse."

"The Lord talks about what one sows, what they will reap, but then goes on to tell us, and I'm paraphrasing—we give what we decide. The 'give' here is time, talent, resources. Always remember, God loves a gleeful giver in whatever you do. Thus concludes today's sermon."

"I've never heard it put in those terms, but it makes sense. And, I'll do my best to keep my wife on the straight and narrow. No more Cantaloupes for her. Unless it's the fruit. If she knows what's good for her."

"Larry, if the Early Birds are still on the road when I decide to retire in five years, I'm buying an RV and joining your caravan. My wife will need a little more convincing, but after I tell her this story, she'll have me quitting tomorrow."

"I'll be following behind all of you," Greg added.

"We need to scoot before our wives think the church is holding us for ransom." Ben chuckled.

"Then we better pray."

Ben smiled as the pastor prayed a blessing over their upcoming travels. *Yes, Lord, thank you for this church. Bless their socks off too. As they've done us.*

~~~

After Rosie's surprise presentation, Betsy and her two friends got back into the car and Bets leaned over the front seat. "Okay, Rose, your driving solves one of the mysteries, but the story you shared last night—you are so full of turtle soup your eyes are turning gree—"

"It's the truth."

"What?" Betsy wanted to go back into the dealership and ask if they had a Q-tip. Obviously wax build-up obstructed her hearing.

"Ladies, it's the God-honest truth."

A chuckle came from the passenger's seat. "I'm sorry I'm laughing, but did you ever think about the man you gave those coupons to? He's imparted the story to everyone who will listen. You're responsible for his income tripling."

"Well, I hope so. I've been praying for him since we met the other day."

"Rosie, I'm not doubting you, but I can't believe you did this by yourself. All of it."

"I can't either, Bets. Without the Lord pushing me out the door. Past my fears. I'd still be wallowing in them at the RV. I'm glad He gave me the strength to face them and move forward. Literally." Rose snorted.

"Amen, but I have to ask. Who gave you the ability to hand a man, standing on a street corner, questionable food coupons? Not seeing that the Lord in heaven had much to do with your dicey transaction."

"He had His hand in this one too. But Mary, I must say, you're spending way too much time with the person sitting in the back seat. Her sassiness is rubbing off on you. In not a good way."

"Rosie, she's caught on quick. And isn't she adorable?" Betsy squeezed Mary's shoulder.

"She is and speaking of sassy. How about we swing by Sassy Seconds *Two*. It's been a while."

"Let's go." Betsy snatched the pillowcase off the seat beside her. "I'm wearing this number in to see if Everly can match a pair of shoes for me."

"See what I mean, Mary? It's hopeless."

"Oh, Rosie, I forgot to tell you." Betsy made a motion with her hands as if she drove. "You aced the track in the Class C today. Congratulations on your superb driving. Larry will be thrilled."

"Thank You, Jesus. There is hope for our friend after all. Now, if you're ready, I'm taking off."

"Oh, Lord, have mercy."

"I take it all back. She's impossible. And if you know what's good for you, don't tell Larry about me driving. I want it to be a surprise."

CHAPTER SEVEN

"Glad you're back, ladies. We're about to start the shortest Early Birds meeting in history. All of us have lots to do, if we're pulling out of Ft. Myers tomorrow." Ben folded one of their chairs and opened his side compartment.

"I'll make the meeting even shorter." Betsy grabbed the other lawn chair. "What Rosie told us last night is true. That's all the input this female has to add on the matter of anything travel."

Ben dropped the chair he held and gawked at Larry and Jeff. Floored and stunned explained the look on their faces. He then reached down and collected what he'd dropped and said, "Anyone else want to elaborate?"

"Nope. Betsy covered it. Let's get cracking." Rose swooped in and snatched the checkered tablecloth off the picnic table, which belonged to Ben and Betsy. She folded it and placed it inside her RV compartment and closed the door.

Then she, Betsy and Mary scurried around their campsites as if someone had hit the fast-forward button.

Ben wanted to stop them, but their busyness achieved more than any instruction he'd give them. *So much for our meeting.* "Oh, I guess we accomplished it. Sort of."

"What did we sort of do?"

"Getting things done."

"Hey, you told us we had tons to do."

"I did and I have stuff to do inside too." Ben climbed the stairs into their RV and Bets followed. "Hon, the bombshell you dropped got things moving. As I asked out there, you want to expound on your earlier statement?"

"I plead the fifth."

"Those words only work in the Senate. Not here at the Stevenson's compound. We don't keep secrets from the other. Do we?" Ben started to tickle Bets, knowing full well the information locked inside her pretty head would be forthcoming.

"Quit. You're upsetting Matilda." Betsy chuckled as she hurried around the kitchen island.

"I am not. Our pooch is fast asleep on the loveseat." Ben came over to where his wife stood and started again.

"You can tickle me all you want. All I'm saying is Larry, Jeff, and you, my beloved, are going to be shocked. Tomorrow morning will be almost like Christmas for one of the Early Birds, but I'm not saying which one."

"Sounds like we better get busy and finish packing. I did always love the night befo—"

Betsy stopped Ben's blabbering with a kiss then said. "Honey Bunch, you'll understand all of this in the morning, but for right now, there's no time for reminiscing. Let's get cracking. Oh, I almost forgot, we're going to Mom's for dinner tonight."

"Supper at Fran's. Yep, that's incentive to get me moving."

"Thought so. Might want to text Larry and Jeff the latest newsflash."

Ben did what his wife suggested and within seconds he received his friend's responses and they made him laugh. Both Larry and Jeff asked him the same question, "Can we leave now?"

"Are you going to spend all day on your phone?"

"Nope. I'm trying to convince our friends to stay on task. For me, I'm leaving you so I can work my magic outside. While I'm doing that, you can batten down the hatches in here. Later, I'll yell for you to help me hook up the truck."

"Okeedokie."

"Matilda, you want to come out and help me?" Their pooch leapt off the loveseat and made it to the door before Ben had her leash in hand. He attached it and said, "Mats, I'm still hoping one day your mama will spring out of bed that quick when I call her name."

"Keep hoping. Now go get busy."

"Yes, ma'am."

Ben hooked Matilda to her cable and watched Larry as he ambled over to their RV spot. His confused stare confirmed he hadn't found out any more from Rosie than Ben had with Betsy on whatever was going to happen in the morning.

"Don't know what it is, Lar, but Betsy says it'll be worth the wait."

"I've never known my wife to keep quiet on anything."

"There's always a first time, but can you believe her

story is true?"

"No. I almost want to find the man and ask if it truly happened."

"Unless Rose can give us his location, I don't think that's possible. We'll have to take her word for it." Ben wanted to laugh, but instead, he added. "And, you'll keep a closer watch of what your wife does on her next Haphazardly Handing out Hospitality."

"Oh, you can count on it." Larry looked at Ben. "And, I can't believe you remembered the name of Rose's new project."

"I can't either, but we better finish up out here." Ben walked to his truck and lowered the tailgate then when he spied his friend looking at him, he put his hand up to his ear and said, "Larry, did you hear that?"

"What are you talking about?"

"Fran's food. It's telling me to get over there now."

"You've sealed the deal, Benjamin. I'm traveling with a bunch of zany people."

~~~

Betsy jumped out of bed the next morning and threw on the same clothes she'd worn the day before. For once she hadn't dropped anything on her shirt while eating her mother's fabulous cooking.

Sadness lingered from their goodbyes, but this morning's activities would keep her mind occupied and her eyes riveted on her friend, Rose Wilford, and the unveiling of her stupendous surprise.

An hour later, Rosie climbed behind the wheel of their Class C. She rolled down the window and shouted for the next county to hear, "I am rootin' tootin' and ready to parlay the pavement."

"Rosebud, unless you're driving us to Daytona—

your antics aren't one bit funny. You can see I'm not laughing?"

"For once I'm not trying to be humorous. Get in here, ya old poop, and I'll tell you all about it."

"No, you're going to tell us all about it now. Make it quick. We've got two-hundred and twenty miles to cover today."

"She took driving lessons. We found out about it yesterday. And, Larry, she's good," Betsy answered for her friend. If she hadn't, they'd still been standing there until the third Thursday of July.

"Like I said, jump in and I'll fill you in." Rose waved a piece of paper out of the window. "Come see my certificate. They gave it to me to prove I'd mastered their challenging class. I suggested they also put down I conquered my fears with every turn I made on the track."

Larry walked the short distance to their RV and appeared to look at the paper. "Ben. Jeff. You need to get over here and see this. It says it right here in black and white. My wife can officially drive our RV. I'll be."

Ben whistled after he checked out the piece of paper Larry held in his hand. "Rosie, I'm impressed."

"From what I've read on Facebook, it's a tough course. Don't know if I'd pass it." Jeff gave Rose a thumbs up.

Betsy appreciated Jeff and Ben's accolades, but wanted to giggle at Larry. He stood holding the certificate, his mouth open. Every few seconds, or so, he'd look up at Rosie, and then back down to the paperwork. Finally, he found words and uttered, "I'm shocked."

"You haven't seen my driving. I'd save those words for when it happens."

Betsy hugged her friend through the window. "I'm so proud of you, but I'm going to make a suggestion since I'm an expert on driving. Why don't you let Larry get us on the road? When we're through town, we can pull over and the open road will be your palette to paint."

"You spent way too much time in Estes Park. Girl, the mountain air got to you."

"I agree with Betsy." Larry opened the driver's door. "Come on out, dear. This certificate tells me that you'll be driving. And I'm a happy man. Thank you."

Rose stepped out and gave Larry a big smacker right on the lips. "You are welcome. And don't you forget it. First chance you have to pull over. I'm ready."

"And before you get in your RV, Rosie, you better hug all of us. Do I have to remind you Larry doesn't want to stop before he has to?" Betsy embraced her friend.

"Amen." Larry got in the driver seat. "We're on the road again."

CHAPTER EIGHT

ON THE ROAD AGAIN

Ben followed Larry and Jeff out of the campground where they'd spent the winter. As the Early Birds made their way to I-75, he thought about his friend, Joe. He'd gone over to see him after they'd left Fran's the night before. He assured the older man they'd be back in the fall.

"Hon, what's with all the smiles this morning?"

Ben conveyed his conversation with Joe to his wife. "Bets, I think the only reason he likes me is for my cooking skills."

"Can't blame him. It's kind of how I feel." Betsy laughed.

"Is that right?"

"Not really, I love you for so many other things than your cooking. Which reminds me, gotta text Mom."

"Breaker 21, are we up to singing our song today?"

Ben heard a loud, scraping noise then Larry's voice came on, "I'm not in on this. She grabbed the mic when

I was sleeping."

Another noise met Ben's ears and it sounded like a snort, but it came from Larry this time. "Lar, are you okay?"

"I think I almost swallowed my tongue."

"Settle down, and no sleeping when you're driving. Okay?"

Betsy leaned over towards Ben. "Hon, keep the mic on. Rosie, let's sing."

Again a racket, disguised as *On the Road Again,* came out of their CB and on Ben's right. Matilda jumped out of her bed and came to the front and looked at her mom. Her headed tilted from side to side.

"Can't blame you, Mats. It hurts my ears too."

Betsy reached across and slapped his arm. "Be nice. We've sung it, and it's official – we're on the road AGAIN."

Ben put the mic in its holder and took a quick peek in his rearview mirror at their 5th wheel. He didn't know when the habit started, but after the rough roads they'd been on—he wanted to see if the RV made the trip with them and the truck.

"You're a smiling fool today. What's up this time?"

"Always enjoy the journey."

"Ben, you're brilliant. I've been looking for a tagline and you found it for me. Always Enjoy the Journey. Yep, I'm writing it down. Then I'll put it in my proposal and it's almost ready to send. One thing is still missing. The title. You need to work your magic on it, as well."

"I'll get on it after I quit driving."

When Ben stole a look at his wife, she indeed wrote something on the pad of paper she'd taken from the side pocket. He wanted to ask her what took her so long since he'd only said four words, but he waited until she put the pen in her lap.

Again Ben glanced in Betsy's direction and when she quit writing and wore a huge grin, he said, "Hon, I hope it was my words that made you a Happy Camper."

"They did. I can't tell you how much I enjoy our brainstorming sessions."

"Don't think we were plotting anything, but I'm *always* glad to help," Ben stressed the one word and Betsy laughed.

"Benjamin Stevenson, so many words want to spill forth on that topic of help, but we know the Lord Almighty took us - two fools – and straightened us out. And He gave me my wonderful, sweet, adorable husband back."

"Go on believing that and we'll celebrate many more anniversaries."

"I'm counting on it." Betsy stuffed the notebook in the side pocket. "So, what did you think of Rosie's news?"

"Both pieces of news surprised me. Don't know which I'd pick to take top billing."

"All I know, there's plenty of chattering going on in the Wilford's RV."

"Hum, I wonder if there's a way to rig the CB to listen in on someone's conversation?"

"Ben, that's illegal, and I can't believe you'd even suggest it. But it is a thought. Can you imagine what we'd hear? They'd give me plenty to write about."

He laughed, but the construction in front of him on I-75 stalled their conversation for about ten miles. Ben had to remind himself, more than once, getting riled at how the different states worked on roads didn't solve the issue at hand.

The narrower lanes and the abundant traffic on Friday morning kept his full attention. As soon as they passed Tampa, the FDOT sign told them they'd run out of construction. Ben also hoped for fewer vehicles when the road opened up.

So much for making good time.

Bets seemed to sense his agitation and stayed quiet. In the stillness, Matilda inched over to Betsy's lap and Ben laughed when their pooch nudged his wife's hand, wanting a pet. Soon enough, he passed the last orange pylon and their conversation resumed.

"We can't bug their trailer, Ben, but we can talk about what our friend has been up to lately."

"I thought talking about people was a sin?"

"It is, but in our case – it's classified as a group discussion. Me. You. And Matilda. We're discussing possible scenes for my next book."

"Guess that makes everything okay, especially when a pooch is involved."

"Yessiree. Now about Rosie and her Hospitality Hazards—"

"It's Haphazardly Handing out Hospitality."

"Okay. Anyway, if her story is true, no person on this planet is safe from her. Next thing she'll do is tackle someone at a parking meter. "No, please, I want to put quarters in the slot for you. Today's your lucky day. I'm the H.H.H. ambassador.'"

"And we'll be standing there cheering her on. Relax, Bets. Larry won't let her antics get out of hand."

"All I'm saying, it's one thing for us to help out churches in the towns we land in. That's safe and can't get us arrested. But accosting people on the street—it's a life sentence waiting to happen. Or at least ten to twenty years."

Ben almost had to pull their rig over to dry the tears blinding him. He grabbed a tissue and wiped his eyes. "Betsy, we're not going to get arrested. But I have to say, when you exaggerate, you go up and over the wall. Grand slam all the way."

"Glad I can amuse you, but I'm telling you - my readers wouldn't believe a word I wrote of a woman on the latter side of sixty doing what she did."

"Bets, in this day and age, people don't think anything of someone buying a gift card at a place like Cantaloupes and giving it to..." Laughter took over again and talking became impossible.

Larry's voice came on the CB at that moment. Ben tried to say something, but ended up handing the mic to Betsy.

"Ben's incapacitated. May I help you?"

"We're taking the next exit. It's time for lunch."

"We'll follow you in. Watch out for the poles."

"Bets, tell your husband he's not funny."

"He already knows it," Ben answered before his wife. "Bye."

Ben pulled into the gas station parking lot, parking next to Jeff. No light poles in sight for any of them to hit on their way out.

"Hon, you want to open the front vent? Think we need to turn the fan on for girly."

After Ben set their trailer's comfort level for Matilda and telling her, "we'll be right back," they headed down the stairs and crossed the parking lot with their friends.

"All I'm going to say is, in my next life, I want to come back as your pooch."

"You'd be so lucky and for the record, Jeff, this is the only life you got. Live it well. And if you'd like, you can refer to me as Oh Wise One. Or Yoda. Whichever you prefer."

"Neither." Jeff opened the door and the Early Birds filed into the Mexican restaurant.

They placed their order and in record time they'd called their numbers. Ben and Betsy picked up the trays for everyone at their table. Not waiting for them, Ben took his seat and unwrapped his burrito and took a bite. At the same time, Rose bowed her head.

"Sorry, Rosie, I'll wait next time."

"It's okay, the Lord understands," Rose started praying, but something seemed to take a hold of her in the middle. She started to pray a verse out of Galatians. "Lord, please give us more of your love, joy, peace, patience, kindness,—"

"And more of my burrito with green chili." Ben's laughter almost made him choke on the second bite he'd slipped in after the prayer began.

"Father forgive Benjamin Stevenson, for he knows not what he does. Or I hope he doesn't. And give him an extra measure of self-control. Amen!"

~~~

Betsy and the other Early Birds walked out of Taco Bell after lunch. They'd almost reached their RVs and Bets asked, "Rosie, what happened in there? You didn't bushwhack anyone with your benevolence."

"You forgot what I named it, didn't you?"

"I did and I don't even remember the initials." Betsy recited the alphabet in her head.

"It's H.H.H., and for your information, no one caught my fancy to do any acts of anything on them."

"Other than my hubby." Betsy laughed when she remembered her friend's prayer.

"Him interrupting me while I'm asking the Lord to bestow the fruits of the Spirit on us. Heaven forbid."

"And, Mrs. Wilford, I'll do it again when my burrito is sitting under a ceiling fan getting frostbite. Are we ready to go?"

Mary walked up. "We are, but I wanted to make sure I gave Rose a big hug before her maiden voyage."

"My Rosie isn't driving on these roads." Larry sauntered past them and unlocked the driver's door."

Betsy stood close enough to feel the heat generating off of her friend after her hubby's comment. And she reached out and grabbed Rose's arm to stop her, or she'd have wrestled Larry out of the front seat—in less time than it took to say 'hallelujah'.

"Rose, you saw the traffic and construction after we left Ft. Myers. Don't think you want to chance running into a concrete barrier or something even worse on your first excursion." Betsy didn't want to mention the pictures of accidents she'd seen posted on Facebook.

"I hate when you two are right, but I'm driving. Soon. Or I'm going to forget what Aaron taught me."

This amused Betsy and she said, "I'm surprised you didn't invite him along. You're always telling people to join us. 'The more the merrier.'"

Rose blushed, "I did. He said he'd love to, but, and I'm quoting here, 'Nancy and the kids. They'd miss me.'"

"You are amazing, Rosie."

"Glad you finally noticed."

"Betsy, give Mary and Rose a hug and let's get on with it." Ben held his keys out in front of him.

"Hon, hold on, I have to tell them what you came up with on our trip here." Betsy looped her arm through his. "My hubby gave me the tagline I needed and it is advice the Early Birds live out every day. Always Enjoy the Journey." She stopped and stared at Ben.

"What have I done now?" Ben stepped closer to his truck.

"Nothing, but I think you also came up with the title. Oh my goodness. It's perfect."

"Since Ben's on a roll, how about our RVs get on one too? I'd like to get to Daytona in the daylight."

Larry started his Class C and left the Early Birds standing in the middle of the parking lot. Everyone, excluding Rose, laughed. He then moved to the wide open spaces. Betsy took a hold of Rosie's arm again when she saw him weave back and forth in the RV.

"Glad he didn't invite me for that ride." Rose unclasped Betsy's hand from her forearm and yelled in the direction of their RV. "Larry, quit fooling around and get yourself over here. Can't you see we're ready?"

"Yes, I can. Jump in when I drive by." Larry yelled back.

"If you're not careful, Baby and I will ride with Mary and Jeff."

"Lar, it's your turn to lead, but pick up your wife. I don't have room for her." Jeff climbed into his Class C.

Betsy smiled when Larry stopped to pick up Rose. Her friend ambled to his side of the vehicle and gave him a kiss. She then walked over to her side and got in. Lar moved to the front of the caravan and took off for I-75.

CHAPTER NINE

"Breaker 21, we're exiting in about three miles. We'll make a left to go to the Springdale RV Park."

"Roger, oh I mean, Larry." Ben laughed at his own joke, but grimaced when he moved his shoulder. Even though they'd stopped two hours ago, it hurt when he took his right arm off the steering wheel and rotated it forward and back.

"Your old sport's injury bothering you again?"

"Little league was tough. It might have to do with using my brain so much today. Caused it to act up."

"I didn't excel in anatomy in school, but the cerebrum and upper arm are not attached." Betsy raised her arm, appearing to show Ben the errors of his ways.

He stared at Betsy a little too long then realized his exit came sooner than he'd expected. "Hon, keep that pose. Please don't move. I want to check it out when we park at the campground."

"Maybe. Maybe not." Betsy chuckled. "Remember, I have to finish my proposal and send it off. I'm also trying a new pasta salad recipe. Not sure what it'll taste lik—"

"It will taste delicious."

Betsy forgot to end her sentence after 'recipe', but concluded her unsavory comments came less and less. However, one slipped out on occasion. She smiled at her hubby. Without his encouragement and lots of prayers, she'd still let the misguided voices direct how she spoke.

And how Betsy wrote her book, if she allowed them in. Up until she'd found the idea for her latest novel, and comedy ruled the day—her other fiction hollered, "lighten up." Her characters either hated their parents. Or something happened to the child, scarring him for life.

"Bets, I don't know if you're aware of this, but we've landed and Ben backed you into your spot. I've been watching as you stared off into space." Rose opened the door. "Must be what Jennifer talked about when she painted up in the Colorado mountains."

"Something like that." Betsy grabbed her purse.

"Here, dear, let me help you out since I haven't done a kindness yet today. You'll be my first recipient."

"I'm honored you chose me and didn't find a boy scout to help across this busy street." Betsy pointed to her left at the road next to the RV Park. "I've got it, maybe when Ben runs to the store later, you can go with him. Help someone carry their groceries out to their car."

"Love it. I'm taking it for action."

"Rosie, they'll try to give you a tip."

"Fine with me. I'll add it to my good will fund. If either of you feel an urge to contribute, I'll make note of your generosity."

"Let's bring it up at our next meeting."

"Which is taking place later tonight," Ben announced on his way by. "That's if my wife gets her work done. Hint. Hint."

"I'm on it. Matilda, you want to help me put the finishing touches on my book proposal?"

"Put Willie Nelson's new CD on and it'll get you going in no time."

Betsy let Matilda out of the back of the truck. Their pooch shot up the stairs of their RV and she followed and opened the door. The minute she shut it, procrastination set in. With bells on.

The bungies on the cabinets beckoned her to remove them since they didn't need them anymore to stay closed. The pan she'd set in the sink broadcast the pasta needed to boil. Did she hear Ben call her to help him outside?

Sit down, Betsy. Focus.

She complied and opened her computer. Betsy found the asterisks, holding the place for her title. Her fingers danced on the keys as she typed, *Always Enjoy the Journey.* "Yes, yes, yes. I love everything about the name."

After typing the now precious words on her cover page, Betsy scrolled to the next page and inserted the four words next to Tagline. "Done. I can't believe I'm finished. Thank You, Lord."

Betsy moved her curser to the top of Page One and checked each line of her document again. Pasta salad, best friends, and Daytona forgotten for the time it would take her to reread her book proposal.

More than her eyes had scrutinized the text. God bless her writing group from Texas, but Betsy still found an error. Not a glaring one, like giving the main characters a different last name, something she'd almost done on her first read through.

No, this scene said the characters parked their RV in one location at the beginning of the chapter. A mere three pages later, they camped in a completely different state. The distance too far to make in less than a day. Even if they owned a diesel-powered motorhome.

Betsy wanted to laugh at the absurdity of what she'd found, but praised the Lord she'd located it. And fixing the faux pas, she saved the file on the computer and on the thumb drive she carried in her purse.

"Pasta salad, here I come…oh, not so fast, I have to send out my proposal. I'm not putting it off one more day."

Betsy found the publisher's name under Small Presses in Writer's Market. To make sure of the correct name to address her proposal, she'd called Linnstrom-Peterson Publishing two weeks before. The receptionist assured her Kevin Linnstrom would receive it.

Next step: Follow their instructions on how to send them her proposal. Betsy opened a new email and copied and pasted her query into the body and attached her file to it. After one more scan for errors, Betsy declared, "Check. Check. And Double Check."

Betsy's finger loomed over the Enter key, but she stopped. Either the Mexican food she'd consumed at lunch gave her a sudden case of indigestion, or her intuition kicked in and made her sweat like a pig on a spit. She sat back in her chair and peered at the clock. *They're still there.*

She dialed the number and a woman said, "Linnstrom-Peterson Publishing. May I help you?"

"I hope so," Betsy told the person on the other end

her concerns about who to send her proposal to, and added. "Trust me, I'm not usually this paranoid."

"I'm glad you called. Kevin Linnstrom is no longer in the Christian fiction department. Let me see, it's now Mr. Andrew Pickle."

Late Friday afternoon, close to the end of June, Betsy Stevenson found out the Lord existed. Not that she doubted His existence, but today He kept her from making a crack about the man's unconventional name.

Betsy managed to say "thank you" to the receptionist and hung up. Not letting the mirth of the moment postpone her sending her proposal, she deleted the other man's name and put in Mr. Pickle's instead.

So far so good.

One more lookie see and Betsy pressed Enter. "It's gone and my 'baby' is in someone else's hands, which by the way is named Mr. Pickle, and all I can do is wait for the rejec—oh, I mean, acceptance. Help me, Jesus."

~~~

"I know what she's doing in there, but I think it'd be okay if I snuck a peek. I want to ask Betsy if she needs help."

"Come on, Ben, we'll only be in there a minute."

"Rose. Mary, if you want to keep your body parts intact, you'll leave her alo—"

Their RV door flung open, stopping Ben from finishing his sentence. His wife stood on the top step and her expression clicked off a myriad of scenarios in his mind. Most he'd rather not consider on a good day. Rose must have thought the same and kept her distance.

Betsy made it down their stairs and before she touched the ground she announced, "People, I sent my proposal to a man named Mr. Pickle. Pickle. Who's got the P…oh, that's so wrong."

His wife plopped down in the closest lawn chair and Rose and Mary rushed over. Rosie asked, "Do you need me to get you a water?"

"Stay with her. I'll get her a bottle." Ben moved up the steps and in two shakes brought water for everyone and handed one to his wife. He grabbed a lawn chair and positioned it in front of Betsy. "Okay, hon, fill us in on what happened."

Betsy recapped what occurred during her proposal sendoff party. "I'm glad I called them back, but the receptionist now wonders what came over me. My voice, while saying thank you, sounded like a high-pitched yodel and a porcupine fighting in a side alley."

"We wondered what that was." Rose's snorts caused their new neighbors to stare.

"If you don't quiet down, they're going to the front office to report us." Betsy moved her head in the direction of the gawkers.

"Why don't we invite them over for bratwursts?" Ben stood. "We have plenty in the freezer. And Betsy promised me on the way here she was making pasta salad."

"Oops, I forgot."

"Betsy, I'll go get the bag of pasta I have. We'll need it." Mary made a beeline for her RV.

"Let me go find Larry. He'll figure out what to fix for our get-acquainted party. Where is he, anyway?"

"I'm behind you, listening to you planning my life."

"Which reminds me. We're going to Daytona International Speedway tomorrow. I've already signed us up." Rose took a bow.

"See what I mean, Larry. We have to watch her

every minute."

"Seems so, Ben, and next she'll tell us she took care of going to the office and extending our reservations for another day."

"I did and they said we can stay in the same spots." Rose took another bow. "Now I'm going into the RV and see what culinary magic I can put together."

Mary returned with the promised pasta and Betsy sent her to the Wilford's. "Change of plans. Give it to Rosie. She said she's whipping up delightful things in her kitchen. Might as well be the pasta salad too. Ben and I will go over to invite our neighbors to dinner."

CHAPTER TEN

"Ben, what does a person wear to a racetrack?" Betsy inquired the next morning as she flipped the turn-style around in her closet. "My clothes aren't screaming auto racing or NASCAR garb. In any way."

"Jeans. T-shirt. Nothing fancy required."

"Still wondering why Rosie wants to go, but I'm sure it'll be interesting. I'll take notes. Might be a scene in my second book."

Her hubby stopped putting on his shoes and stared at her. "Say what?"

"I have to write a sequel to *Always Enjoy the Journey.* Too many words for only one book."

"Along with Book #2, are you also writing your blogs? Haven't seen one…in months."

"Don't remind me. Traveling around in the RV, writing a novel, and traipsing off to help Mary's niece takes all my time."

"Which brings up that there's no time left for her patient husband. He picks up the scattered pieces the Great American Novelist gives him at the end of the day." Ben lay back on the bed and the deep sigh he expelled sounded as if it came from his toes.

"You are so mistreated, but I will try to open up a minute for you next Thursday."

"So nice of you, dear."

"I do what I can." Betsy continued to search for what to wear, but to no avail. So she leaned into her closet to look at the cubby in the back. Next thing she knew, Ben gave her backend a slight nudge, causing her to almost land on the shelf inside of the tiny room.

His laughter lit Betsy's ire and any self-control she'd gleaned from her quiet time left the building. "Mr. Stevenson, if you're not out of my sight when I get up from in here, you are dead meat."

Betsy righted herself and she found no damage on any part of her, but marveled at the speed her hubby ran out of their bedroom. *Good thing, buster, you go somewhere else. And there better be cof—.*

"Your coffee's on the counter. I'll be outside. I looooooooove you."

"Yea. Yea. Yea. Tell everyone I'll be out in a minute." Betsy ventured to her closet again and chose a blue flowered shirt to wear with her jeans. "Good to go."

Betsy grabbed her coffee and made a stop at her desk to check emails, and write a note to do a blog. No emails from Mr. Pickle, but she stopped and read the short one from her friend, Tina.

"We're doing great. Thanks for your prayers. I'm posting pictures of our second honeymoon on Facebook. Love you!"

Tina's note made Betsy forget her hubby's previous transgression. "Thank You, Lord, for helping another person find out prayer works to save a marriage. I don't know about You, but I will never tire of hearing those stories.

"And if we don't get to the speedway, they'll give our seats to someone else." Rose came in their door. "And how are you this morning, Matilda?"

"She's fine, but not happy we're leaving her." Betsy closed her computer. "Before I forget, I got a note from Tina. She's posting pictures later of their trip."

"Praise the Lord and pass...oh, I forgot. I'm not saying it anymore. Larry informed me the other day I say it too much."

"Rosie, if you quit using your signature saying, and it's in my book, it'll appear we're traveling with a new couple."

"We can't have that. Now let's get a move on. Don't know why, but I'm excited to visit the racetrack. It's as if the Lord is telling me to be aware. Maybe there's an H.H.H. on the Early Birds horizon? Never know."

"Or your I.B.S. is flaring up." Betsy grabbed her coffee and hurried down the steps before her friend sent her tumbling down the same stairs. She'd already had one too many spills for one day.

"Your wit is worrisome, and leave the diagnosing to me. I'm better at it." Rose strolled past her and planted herself in the middle of the front seat of the dually.

Betsy jumped in, taking her seat behind Rosie, and started to tap her friend's arm. "Rose, I'm keeping track, no pun intended, of you today. No funny business, in anything you do, or we're cutting the speedway tour short."

"Wouldn't think of it."

All the way down International Speedway

Boulevard, Betsy doubted her friend's words. But she put the promise of watching Rose away after Ben parked their truck, and she witnessed the outside of the racetrack.

She'd seen it on television, but in person—what an amazing place. Her excitement level soared. Bets latched onto Ben's hand and drug him away from the statues scattered along the walkway. "Dear, hurry up. We need to go get our seats."

Once inside, Ben handed Betsy a ticket and they took a seat in the open-air bus. The tour guide/driver introduced herself as Michelle and she said, "Welcome to Daytona International Speedway. Since the first question is always when the racetrack opened – the answer is 1959."

Michelle drove the track and shared stories of attending the race with her daddy. "He brought me to this spot." She stopped the bus at the Start/Finish line and opened the door. "You have plenty of time. No need to hurry. Don't forget to take tons of pictures while we're here."

Betsy exited and took more than her share of photos of the inside of the iconic landmark. Ben and the other Early Birds walked over to the winner's circle. When she headed in their direction, she met up with Michelle.

"Enjoying yourself?"

"I am. Surprisingly. Didn't know I liked NASCAR."

"If you're like me, something takes ahold of you when you walk through the doors. When I was a kid, Daddy and I hung out here. He worked on the maintenance crew. We got to meet all the great race car drivers."

Betsy waited for Michelle to drop names, but instead, she talked on a different topic, "Daddy's still works here part-time, unless he's fixing up the building for Hands to Help. When it's done, kids in the area will come and learn skills of all kinds."

The information made Betsy want to run and grab the Early Birds, but she left them alone and said, "Michelle, since I don't know what your schedule is, do you have time after our tour to tell us more about your father's project?"

"I'm off after this one. We can talk until the gates close at 5:00."

Lord, thank You for an opportunity to help others and for an idea for my blog.

~~~

"Larry, hand me a hammer. Left mine in the truck." Ben reached out and retrieved the tool then stretched his arms as far up as they'd go and nailed the board in place. "Jeff, you do know I'm not as tall as you?"

"If we're going to continue to help humanity, you might want to invest in a pair of elevator shoes." Jeff's laughter echoed in the empty classroom.

"I talked to Michelle's dad and he's excited about the grand opening. Wished we'd have known. We'd have stayed longer.

"South Carolina awaits." Ben took his arm down and his shoulder ached, telling him not to hold the previous position again. Or not for that length of time.

"FYI. I called the campground where we're staying. It's funny, our reservations didn't start until tomorrow night. Not tonight."

"Larry, do you think Rosie called and changed them?"

"No, the Lord's mysterious ways are at work in our new ministry. It has to be Him. How else does a person find out about this opportunity?"

"Don't know, Lar, but I'm glad we ran into it." Ben walked over to finish nailing in a section of baseboards. He checked the time on the clock. "I hope our wives bring us leftovers for dinner."

"Betsy needs to rename her book. She can call it: *Always Enjoy the Journey—Ben Stevenson's Guide to How Many Times You Can Eat in One Day.*"

"Is that right, Jeff? And since I'm more knowledgeable about the Bible than you are. In the one version I have, it states the Lord gave us our stomachs to be able to feast on the plethora of food He supplies."

"An interesting take on His Word, Mr. Stevenson. Tell me you men are ready to eat."

"Rosie, you'd be correct. If I haven't told you today—you're the best wife I've ever had. Did you bring the pasta salad?"

"I'm the only wife you've ever had. And, yes, I did. We also brought enough sandwiches and chips to feed everyone in a five-mile radius of this place." Rose set out the plates and utensils on the tables. "Betsy's bringing the rest. She must have stopped to talk to Michelle."

"She did and I lightened her load." Michelle came in carrying a large yellow bowl and put it down on the table. Then she did a complete turnaround and said, "You've been busy this afternoon."

"The Early Birds don't waste time. We're get-it-doners."

"Bets, we do get things done, but did you do something with Mary? My wife seems to be missing."

"I sent Mary and the other box of food to the building next door. She'll be right over." Michelle steered the men to the table. "Eat up. I hear there's plenty to go around."

Ben reached for the large bowl, filled with his new favorite. He knew full well he'd have to share it but said, "It's all mine?"

"Hon, set the bowl down." Betsy took the lid off when he did and put the spoon in the salad.

"I've only known you a few hours, but you're all amazing."

"Who's amazing." Mary hurried into the room. "Did she tell you another story about her dad and I missed it?"

"No, she was complimenting us." Rose scooped out an abundant helping of pasta salad and put it on her plate.

"Miss Rose is right. Dad won't recognize the place when he gets here tomorrow. I'm sorry you missed meeting him."

"We are too, but tell him we're praying for Hands to Help. And if you think of it, Michelle, pray for us too. We'd love to find more places like this to help. Don't know about my friends, but I have a bunch of benevolence bubbling inside me. It's—"

"And, before it boils over, Rosebud, bring me a bologna sandwich, and sit your buns down by me."

Larry's uncharacteristic comment cracked Ben up and almost caused him to fling his plate across the room. When he scanned the rest of the group, they appeared to want to do the same.

"Early Birds, I have loved getting to know you." Michelle opened her napkin and placed it on her lap.

"And, you can count on me and my daddy's prayers. We'll pray you continue to have this much fun and your ministry spreads to every corner of the globe."

"Please, oh please, don't give Rosie any ideas, Michelle. There's still more of the USA we want to see and more people to help. After we've touched all of the states, and maybe even Alaska, we'll talk about renting RVs and spreading our wings in the other six continents."

Ben listened to Larry then took out his phone and made a note to check on the cost of renting a super-sized Class A in Europe. *Lord, please prepare the path to wherever You want us to go.*

CHAPTER ELEVEN

Betsy settled in the passenger seat as the Early Birds made their way farther up the East Coast. For whatever reason Johnny Cash's song, *I've Been Everywhere,* started whirling around in her head. No, they hadn't been 'everywhere', but their RVs kept moving after they left Daytona.

And their new ministry continued too. In a restaurant in Georgia, Mary kept staring at a family seated at the next table. Betsy finally said to her, "They are going to think you're stalking them if you don't quit gawking at them."

"Can't help it. Watch them, Bets. Mom and Dad are laughing at whatever the kids are saying. The children are so well behaved. Brings back memories of how people used to compliment my parents when we went out to eat. I want to do the same."

"I'm going out on a limb here, but you're handing out this hospitality. They'd get up and run out of here if a number of senior citizens gathered around their table and gave them kudos on being great parents."

"Good point. Jeff, can you give me all the money

you have in your wallet?"

Betsy chuckled at Mary's request and Jeff's expression, but when he said, "Mary, I only have ten bucks." She wanted to hoot.

"Thanks, dear, but I need more. I'm taking up a collection and I'll tell everyone about it when I get back to the table."

Betsy had never seen a group of people gather monies without knowing where it'd go. In the end, Mary had $99.25. Her friend got up and strolled to the other table. From the look on the couple's face, her gesture touched their hearts.

Mary returned and told the others what she'd shared with Betsy. "I know Jeff thinks I'm nuts to do it, but every time someone praised my parents on a job well done, both of them couldn't quit smiling."

"Like you did right then." Jeff put his arm around Mary. "When I get cash, I'll pay everyone back for the money you gave my wife."

"Nah. This is one more example of how the Early Birds distribute small snippets of the Savior's love everywhere we go."

Betsy smiled at the memory from the night before. And how all of them had embraced the ministries the Lord placed in their path. But, today, her thoughts touched on her writing—the item she questioned every other day. Did she truly hear His calling on it?

"I've watched you off and on the last twenty miles, Bets. You've been all grins then a minute ago it changed. What's that crazy brain of yours doing over there?"

Ben's voice brought her back to their travels. "Do you really want to know?"

"I asked, didn't I?"

Betsy shared with her hubby the highs and lows going on inside her head. "Ben, I don't doubt I'm being anxious for no reason. It is way too soon to expect an answer as to whether they will accept or reject my proposal."

"I don't know much about the publishing world, and as you've said, it changes all the time. But in this case, dear, nothing has changed. Patience is the key in waiting for their answer, or you'll drive yourself nuts."

"And you along with me."

"I'm not saying a word on that subject, but as your book says, the travelers need to always enjoy the journey. How about we start doing more of it and trust the Lord knows what He's doing. Just so you know, He does have this all figured out."

"Like last night, when you and the guys ran to Walmart after dinner?" Betsy chuckled.

"Don't remind me. And, anyway, what happened at Walmart was all Jeff and Larry's fault."

"I'm not sure minute details matter here, but it's going in my next book. Tell me again what happened. I'm going to record it."

"Why?"

"When I'm a New York Best Selling Author, you'll thank me." Betsy took out her phone and pressed the record button.

Ben straightened in the driver's seat. "Larry and Jeff accompanied me to the store. Notice I used a bigger word here. Yes, one of us needed something. No, that part was me. I wanted ice cream. No matter. I've got my signal on to turn into a parking spot and I'm getting ready to turn and Larry yells, "Let the person coming the other direction have it."

I motioned to the woman to take the spot and searched for another one. Do I have to do this, Betsy?"

"It's getting to the good part. Continue." A giggled escaped.

"You laugh one more time and I won't finish."

"Mums the word."

"Anyway, I parked and the three of us walked inside. I took a cart and waited for Larry to clean it with the wipe. As he was doing it, I saw an older woman walk in and decided to give her our cart.

"She took it, but she gave us a look as if to say we're lunatics. Jeff grabbed another cart and again I waited for Mr. Clean to finish his wipe down. We headed to the ice cream aisle and who did we meet— the woman I'd given the cart to?

"We start doing the aisle shuffle and she finally stopped and said, "You gave me your parking spot, and then your 'clean' shopping cart, but now you're following me. If you don't quit being everywhere I am, I'm calling security."

"The three men backed off, which concludes my story. You can turn the recorder off."

She did and said, "Hon, I still can't believe the woman thought the three of you were tailing her. As I said, it's going in Book #2. Publishers will clamor for all my books, if I add stories like this one."

"I hope so. We need extra income since we're handing it out to families in restaurants now."

"Breaker 21, in three miles we'll reach our destination. Looks like we'll make a few turns to get there."

Betsy had pulled up the Wishbone Beach State Park

where Ben made reservations. The site boasted of water-view campsites and spectacular sunsets. *We'll see if they can beat Biloxi, Mississippi.*

While the men checked in, Betsy and Matilda exited the truck and took a seat at the picnic area. A moment later her two friends joined her. Rosie wore a determined look and suggested, "How about we surprise Larry and unhook the car? How hard can it be?"

Betsy didn't have an answer to Rose's question, but moved with her and Mary to the car. Their contemplation must have taken longer than planned because a vehicle pulled next to them. The man said, "Don't want to intrude, but do you want me to tell you a trick I learned in unhooking my own car?"

"Sir, you're not intruding one little bit. And since we'll be working together, my name is Rose. Go ahead. Fire away."

The man got out of his sedan. "Since your car and RV aren't lined up, it'll be easier if you get in your RV and pull forward to straighten it out. I'll tell you when to stop."

"I've got this because I'm an expert driv—"

"Rosie, please get in and spare the man the details of your learning-to-drive story. He's not interested in anything other than helping us unfasten the Blue Ox."

"Ye of little faith. I wasn't going to tell him a thing, Bets."

"I'll believe you when the snow flies in Florida in January."

"Ladies, the man wants to help us." Mary came and stood next to them. "Not hear how crazy we are."

"Sorry." Rose got in and put the window down. She

stuck her head out of it, "I'm ready."

"Take it slow, and straighten out your wheels." The man directed Rose a foot forward. "Perfect. You'll be able to release the arms now."

Rose jumped out and hit the levers then reached down and pulled out the pins. "Sir, you're an angel."

The man waved on his way to his car. When he opened the driver's door, his pooch greeted him as if he'd been gone for days. Betsy grinned and said as the gentleman drove off. "Matilda, you don't bark, but you're always happy to see us, even if we're gone five minutes."

"We've been gone ten and can someone tell me why my RV is out in the middle of the parking lot?" Larry came around the side of his Class C.

"Do I have a story to tell you. Oh, before I do. I forgot to get the man's name."

"Rosie, it's okay. No need to send him a thank you note." Betsy laughed then said, "Don't get perturbed at her, Larry. Rosie wanted to surprise you and have your car freed from its shackles when you came back out."

"Betsy, if writing doesn't pan out—your phraseology will entertain the masses."

"Well, thank you, Mr. Wilford."

"Anytime. Now let's get parked. I hear the sunsets are phenomenal.

~~~

A short time later, Ben hit the button and the automatic jacks came down to rest on the boards he'd set in place on the ground. However, the night before, he'd somehow forgotten to lower the jacks first and started to reach to pull the pin to free the trailer from the truck.

He realized his mistake in time and when his hands quit shaking, he put the jacks down and thanked the Lord for His mercy. Keeping a fool—him—from dropping the 5th wheel on the back of their dually.

One wrong move and Jeff and Larry saw it all. His younger friend suggested, "How about we bring our wives flowers and keep your near-miss under our cowboy hats. You with me on this?"

"I don't wear western wear. Makes me look shorter than I am, but I'm not breathing a word of this to Rosie."

"Me neither. I mean I won't tell Betsy about my close call. Taught me a lesson, though, don't hurry."

"My Rosie says to slow down and smell the petunias. Don't think her advice applies here, but..."

"It does."

Rose and their pooch, Baby, materialized out of nowhere and her two-word agreement had sent the men into a routine reminiscent of the Three Stooges. Ben, as well as the other two, he hoped, held their breath. *What did she hear?*

Her next statement settled Ben's nerves. "Have any of you kept track of all the love we've been giving away. And we can't forget the ones people have done for us. This new ministry is making me giddy."

Not sure if the hippity hop at the end of Rose's statement had an adverse effect on their dog, but Baby started barking and did her best to squirm out of her owner's arms. "Guess Baby isn't feeling it. I'll be taking her in now."

Rose disappeared and Ben exhaled then whispered, "I don't think she heard our conversation about you know what."

"Ben, if she heard anything we said, my wife's head is so full of helping mankind, your monstrosity could fall on her foot and she'd limp away saying, "I can still serve the Lord with one appendage."

After Ben and the other two quit laughing, he said to them, "The Early Birds wouldn't know what to do without Rosie in our lives. She keeps us going on the road in the right direction."

"That she does, Benjamin. That she does."

Ben realized he'd stood outside longer than normal reminiscing and chuckled as he closed his outside compartment. He also thanked the Lord for no more mishaps. The near disaster the night before sat fresh on his mind. He'd prefer never to have a repeat performance.

CHAPTER TWELVE

"Don't know about you, but I've seen way too many side roads," Larry Wilford's voice came over the CB radio.

"I vote we stop at the Visitor's Center once we cross into Virginia. We need to discuss our travel plans."

"I'm with Betsy. What's the best route to Washington, DC.?"

DC? What?

Betsy scanned their atlas as her hubby tooled down the road. She shut it when Ben pulled into the parking lot five miles later. Before she had a chance to open the door, Rose rapped on her window. "Guess we're having an Early Birds meeting right here. Hope they don't mind."

"Excellent idea." Jeff and Mary strolled by. "How about we sit in the shade? It's hot out here."

They decided on a picnic table and Betsy jumped in and began the meeting. "Don't know when we changed course, away from the coast, but pulling three RVs into the nation's capital is: Insane. Impractical. And did I mention…Impossible."

"Betsy, driving our rigs into DC is all three of those, but Mary checked out the Boondocking app on my phone and she found acreage where we can park and it won't cost us a dime."

"The farm is off of 64, about ten miles. I contacted the man in charge and he has spots available. If it's okay with everyone?"

"Mary, you're hired to do our itinerary from here on out, but make sure we see some more cows. It's been a while."

Rose's comment concerning bovines tickled Betsy since they'd seen herds of them along their travels that day. But at the moment, Jeff and Mary garnered her attention. They seemed to squirm when they'd been voted in as their new travel planners.

I'll be asking Mary about this later, but right now there's a more pressing matter. "Jeff and Miss Rose. Neither of you have ever been to DC in the middle to late June, have you? As you notice, it's hot around these parts in the summertime."

"Can't be as bad as Florida, or Texas."

"Oh yes it can, Jeff. Me and one of my partners, where I worked, came here for a meeting years ago. I got overheated and a cadet from Annapolis brought me tons of water to drink to cool me down. I'd never experienced such a scorcher." Betsy wiped a trickle of sweat from her brow.

"My wife is telling me a Navy man saved her life. Funny, I've never heard that story."

"Ben, it was way before your time, I was on a business trip to DC. Back to our discussion, I recommend we stay on the coast. It'll still be warm, but doable. We can hit DC on the way back down to Florida in October or November. Much cooler then."

"All in favor of taking in Washington on the way up, raise your hand." Ben raised his.

Betsy left her arm at her side, while the others voted for a change of locale. She'd loved visiting all the sights years ago, so why argue over a slight detour? Didn't she write by the seat of her pants? Travel should be the same way.

She thought of Johnny Cash's song again. *Pretty sure by the end of this trip, we'll be able to say, we've been everywhere...and then some. And I'll live to write about it.*

Betsy wanted to put in her late vote, but Rosie interrupted her hand movement when she stood up. "Along with DC, since we're going west a little ways, let's add in a hike or two on the Appalachian Trail."

"I've officially heard it all. Rosie, do you know what it takes to trudge the infamous trail through the wilderness?"

"You put one foot in front of the other. What else is there? All I want to do is touch the trail, not hike all 2500 miles of it."

"What a relief. Thought you were going to tell me you wanted to stay overnight, which might have lasted less than a minute. A visit from a mouse in your campsite and you'd be out of there before it asked for cheese."

"Mr. Wilford, enough about rodents and what they eat. I'm simply putting in my suggestion for other places to see while we're on the East Coast. And in the neighborhood of them."

"Rosie, I'd like to see the trail too, but right now

I'm more interested in hearing about my wife's Navy friend."

"Don't recall much about the man, but the uniform pants he wore—I'd like to know how you get such a precise crease in them?"

"Pardon me for eavesdropping, but it takes practice, ma'am. Lots of practice."

Betsy stared at a young man in uniform and words she'd known a second ago escaped her. Thankfully the other five stumbled all over themselves to acknowledge his service in the military.

"Thank you. I'm from a family who have always served in the Navy. Never a doubt I'd follow them and make it a career. Like my father and grandfather." He pulled out his wallet. "These are also the reason why I'm staying in."

Betsy stared at the dark-haired woman and the two little girls sitting on her lap. The man who showed them the picture posed next to his wife in the professional photo. Their matching smiles spoke of their love for each other.

"Can I get in to see too? My friends seem to think all of us are tall."

The man stepped over to Rose and handed her his wallet. "This is Colleen. The twins are Trina and Tricia. Don't know how it happened." He chuckled. "I'm Daniel. Friends call me Danny."

"Mine is Rose, and I'm pretty sure you've figured out where babies come from by now."

"Yes, we have, ma'am. The twin part has us baffled. Both our moms checked the ancestry site and neither family ever had multiples. Colleen's mother said her line carried her clear back to the early 1800s.

Didn't find a one."

"Whatever your family history, sounds like the Lord wanted you two as the parents to those special little girls."

"That's the only answer we've come up with and we're trusting Him to help us raise them. I know we'll talk a lot when the girls start dating."

"Son, they're still toddlers. Enjoy them now. You've got a while before they turn sixteen." Larry stood. "Now it's time for us to hit the road."

"Where are you headed?"

"We're parking our RVs in Virginia then sightseeing in and around Washington."

"But first, my dear sweet hubby, we're walking the Appalachian Trail."

Betsy glimpsed the serviceman's bewilderment and decided to intervene. "Danny, this is where my friend is talking complete nonsense. She doesn't hike and none of the rest of us do either." Betsy chuckled while she stared at Rose.

"Ladies, Daniel does not want to hear about the Early Birds fitness abilities, or lack thereof." Larry laughed.

"Sir, I'd love to spend a day with all of you. Sounds like you're a fun group of people to run around with."

"We are. Hey, Bets, give our new friend one of your business cards. You can stay in touch, and send us pictures of your girls."

"Danny, we need to get going." Another man in uniform came up to them at the picnic table.

"Thank you both for your service." Ben reached out his hand.

"Hold the handshakes. I'm a hugger."

Betsy felt sorry for Danny and the other man after Rose got ahold of them. When their faces held a "help me" expression, she moved in. "Rosie, if you're not careful, they'll ask you to sign up to fight the war on terror."

"With a grip like hers, you could squeeze the detainees and they'd give us a full statement." Danny's commanding officer chuckled.

The men walked away and Betsy witnessed Rose as she sprinted up to them. In a matter of minutes, their heads bowed and her requests heavenward, in the middle of a parking lot, echoed for all to hear.

"These men will never be the same after meeting us."

"No, they won't, Larry, but I think they'll remember Rose the most."

"Bets, at every stop Rose leaves her mark. And today the Lord blessed two servicemen. They need everything we can give them. Especially prayers."

~~~

"Bets, I don't know about you, but I'm not sure I'd call our meeting with Danny as helping humanity. I do know one thing; it was a pleasure spending time with him."

"As Rose said when we finished hugging, 'we're the keeper of kindness'."

"Our friend and her comments are a Hallmark card waiting to happen." Ben laughed.

"Remind me to tell her what you said."

"Not a chance. She'll come after me with one of her hugs and I'm not in the mood to jog today."

"Rosie darting around leaves a lasting impression, doesn't it? Wish I'd have videotaped it."

"Got an idea. We elected Jeff and Mary as our tour guides, how about you become our videographer?"

Betsy raised her hand. "I accept. And while we're on the subject of the Miller's, did you see how they reacted to them becoming our tour guides?"

"I didn't see anything out of the ordinary. I'm zeroed in on what you or Rosie do. At any given time. I don't notice what else goes on around me."

Betsy filled him in on what she'd seen. Even to him it seemed strange, but he'd count on his wife to find out the details. If she failed, she'd send in Rosie. Her hugs made people squeal.

"Breaker 21, we're about a mile from the farm. Mary called and they're waiting for us to arrive."

Ben turned down the gravel road five minutes later and stopped behind Larry. Jeff jumped out and talked to a younger man. Mid-thirties at the most. When they finished, Jeff pointed in the direction of a field and they moved their RVs to the designated spots.

"You didn't tell us we'd have full hook-ups." Ben shut the door to the power receptacle. "I can't believe this set-up."

"Welcome. I'm Patrick Davis. We had high aspirations for this section of land. Talked about setting up a full-fledged RV Park, but when we finished this row, we decided to keep it on a smaller scale. Give RVers a place to pull in."

"RV spots around here will eat your lunch."

"Jeff, that's why we signed up with the boondocking site. The idea of free appeals to most everyone."

"We'll see about 'free'. A piece of property this size, you have to have work for all of us to do around here."

"Ben's right. Please make us a list of things we can do while we're parked."

"Didn't expect this, Jeff, but there is the fence the cows tried to knock down the other day."

"Hey, Rosie, here's your chance to see a herd of your favorite animals."

"Looking forward to it and it's another opportunity for the Early Birds to Haphazardly Hand out Hospitality."

"While Rosie's ogling at another herd of cattle, we'll be working on the downed fence?" Ben opened his side compartment and came out with a hammer.

"Speak for yourself. I don't want to work." Larry laughed.

CHAPTER THIRTEEN

"**B**en, you need to get down here." Betsy scrolled through her emails the next morning and blinked as she clicked on the one from Lindstrom-Peterson Publishing.

"What's all the yelling about? Poor Matilda is under the table shaking."

"Sorry, buddy, but Ben you have to see this." Betsy stayed planted at her desk, but wanted to jump around their 5th wheel, doing a happy dance.

Ben ambled down the two stairs and made his way over to Betsy's desk. "Okay, dear, what has you so excited? Did we win the lottery we never play?"

She opened the email and read,

"Dear Betsy Stevenson:

We've reviewed your book proposal. Please send your full manuscript. Your comedy and the storyline of RVing couples intrigued me and our staff who read it. We also think there's a sequel (or two) with this theme in mind. Personally, I can't wait to read the rest of the story.

As a small publishing house, we're looking for a twist on the ordinary. *Always Enjoy the Journey* is it.

Betsy, all I can say is hold onto your hat. I'm certain our committee will push it through and will want your novel published by August.

Kevin or myself will be in touch. Welcome to the Linnstrom-Peterson Publishing family!

Mr. Andrew Pickle

Editor, Linnstrom-Peterson Publishing

Betsy stared up at her husband and his shocked expression prompted her to say, "I can see you are as surprised as I am about this piece of news."

"I don't know what to say other than, WOW! And from what you've said to me over the years, this doesn't happen to most writers."

"You're absolutely right and I'm almost thinking I need you to shake me 'cause I'm still under the covers asleep. But since it's such a sweet dream, don't wake me."

"No, dear, you're awake and it sounds like your life has taken an interesting turn."

"It's *our* life, Benjamin. You are part of this ride called writing. I'll need someone to take care of the business end. I'll be too busy with pen in hand, writing Book Two, Three,—"

"Sorry, hon, I'm retired. But if you sweeten the pot and give me a title. Say, CEO of Marketing and Daily Operations, we might have a deal."

"Done." Betsy stood and gave Ben a hug then took a step back. "Hon, I can't believe this. I only sent them the proposal three weeks ago."

"When the Lord wants something done, He doesn't waste time. I suggest you sit down and send them what they ask for." Ben tapped on the back of her office chair.

"I will, but first I have to tell the others. They're a part of this and gave me tons of material for the book." Betsy laughed on her way to the door, but stopped to talk to their pooch. "Matilda, I'll give you a special t.r.e.a.t. later to celebrate."

Their dog's ears perked and she darted out of her hiding place, jumping around like her fur caught fire. Instead of delaying her special goodie, Betsy strolled around the counter and got a bone out. "Yes, I'll learn one of these days not to mention that word."

"I doubt it and I'm as bad as you. You ready to invite the Wilford's and Miller's over? As the note said, 'Hold onto your hat.' When Rosie hears the good news, she's bound to bowl you over with enthusiasm unmatched by any we've seen before."

Ben's words and then some happened after the two couples entered their RV and Betsy uttered the words "the publisher sounds interested". Rose raced over and gave Betsy an exuberant hug.

Her boisterous behavior leveled off and Rosie raised her arms, high above her head, and declared, "Girlfriend, I've blabbed for months about how stupendous your crazier-than-a-loon writing is."

"Mr. Pickle referred to it as 'humor', but I do agree it's the nuttiness surrounding me that sets the book apart from others out there."

"The Early Birds come through again. Congratulations, my dear." Mary came over and hugged Betsy when Rose moved away.

"Ditto to what my wife said. Great news. Is this one of those times we can say, 'We knew you when?'"

"When, or if this happens, I'm hoping all of you come with me to the book signing. I want everyone to meet my cronies in crime."

"Larry, are you asleep over there? Haven't heard you say anything to Bets."

"I'm letting everyone have their moment." He smiled then put in his two cents, "Congratulations Betsy. I do have one question. When you hit the New York Bestseller List, will you still make your potato salad for us? You won't let fame take it off our plates, will you?"

"Our bestest friend has gotten important news and you're thinking of a food item. And, it's a poor pun, if I may say so myself."

"I want to make sure Bets will still associate with us. Oh, and still share her culinary delights."

"Hon, since we're celebrating your great news, how about I take you to the store and you whip up a batch. We'll make a party out of this."

"Ben, I'm aghast you'd ask me such a thing. I might hurt my fingers. You know me around knives. To be safe, you better call our insurance man. Up the bodily injury policy on me. My hands are more valuable. As of today."

"Her humility needs work, but I'm so proud of you, Bets. It's taken a lot of years, but the Lord's timing. It's perfect."

"Thanks, sweetie." Betsy decided instead of going down memory lane, she'd head them in another direction. "I don't know about the rest of you, but going to Washington, DC will help in my research for my next book. I'll pack my notebook for those moments any of you act up."

"We'll start behaving now that we know you're documenting our every move." Jeff moved to the door.

"Mary, let's go before you or I do something Betsy puts in an upcoming novel."

Betsy wanted to make a comment about the Miller's questionable behavior the day before, but let them walk out the door. Larry and Rose followed close behind.

"Hold on. I'm checking the train schedule. It leaves at 10:45. Arrival into DC is at 12:00. We can see the sights and celebrate Betsy's big news. Let's meet at the dually in five minutes."

"Make it ten, Benjamin. It will give Betsy more time to gawk at her email a dozen or more times."

"Rose, that's a given. Ten it is. We'll still have plenty of time to make it to the train on time."

Betsy followed her friend's suggestion and for the next minute or so, she savored the joy the email evoked. *Thank You, Lord!*

"Don't want to rush you, hon, but are you about ready?"

Ben's voice almost made Betsy teeter a bit on her office chair. "I am, but next time you see me in deep thought, don't yell in my ear. Anyway, I'm checking to make sure I wasn't imagining it."

"You weren't. It's true and in black and white."

"And, it's going to take me a while to absorb the news." Betsy stood and grabbed her purse off the top of the desk.

Ben walked over and opened the door. "Don't forget, they said they wanted the rest of your manuscript? Sooner than later."

"I'll do it when we get back tonight, and after I glance through my manuscript again."

"For the twentieth time."

"Twenty-first." Betsy laughed, but in truth she'd hit

a number closer to nine or ten times of actually rereading it. "Don't worry Ben, I promise to let it go…that is…when it's perfect." She scooted past her hubby and scurried down the stairs to their truck. "Yep, when it's flawless."

~~~

Betsy locked the door, after she'd gone back to get her phone, and the Early Birds hit the road. About halfway to the Metro rail station parking lot, she announced, "If Ben doesn't mind, how about we drive in? It's mid-week. Parking won't be a problem."

Famous last words. Even with navigation, the ability to park and signage sent them around the same building three times. On the third time, Betsy voiced her opinion, "Don't know what P.I.T.S. is doing, but I'm ready to toss her out the window. Oh, now she's 'recalculating'."

"Since I'm the driver, where is she 'recalculating' us to?"

"The Pentagon. I Googled it while you two discussed the recent de ja vu. Any minute MapQuest will give you the directions you need," Larry talked, but his phone remained silent.

"There will be a big sign telling us which exit to take."

Betsy prayed Mary's assessment of large signs came true since they'd been a problem in their travels so far that day. All seemed on track until she saw a teeny tiny sign. Bets yelled, "Ben, you need this exit."

Her hubby somehow moved over the two lanes and made his way down the off-ramp. Mario Andretti must have replaced Ben behind the wheel. When he reached the stop sign, and all four wheels touched the pavement,

Betsy stared at her hubby. Speechless.

Signage plagued them once again. At the Pentagon, every spot indicated only vehicles with specific stickers could park there. But, since Betsy saw other people getting out of their cars who appeared like tourists, she reasoned they'd do it too.

"I hope you're right, dear."

"I am. Come on, let's get this party started." Betsy took off out of the truck and linked arms with Rose and Mary. They headed in the direction of the octagon structure, until Bets stopped. "Wait a minute, we need to do a selfie."

Bets clicked the button on her phone to take the photo. While she held it up, she fluffed her hair. The other two needed to tend to theirs too, but Mary appeared more interested in tugging on Betsy's arm than posing for a picture.

"What in the world do you want?"

Her younger friend pointed. "Bets, the sign over there says, 'No cameras allowed.' And, poli—"

"Police cars are at nine and noon."

"I'm copying the obvious, Rose." Betsy watched the officer to their left get out of his car. The other one, parked in front of them, stuck his index finger out of the window. He motioned for anyone of them to come over to his car.

Not wanting either officer to take out his Taser, or give the men in blue a reason to draw their firearms, Betsy hurried over to the patrol car in front of them. She also kept her eyes on the other one and yelled to him, "Sir, this policeman wants to see us, too. We'll get back to you."

The officer must not have understood Betsy's

explanation since he kept coming towards them. She tried again, but this time Bets pointed down at the patrol car she stood next to with gusto. Finally, he turned and strolled back to his car.

Her breathing resumed and Betsy's full attention zoomed in on the policeman sitting in his vehicle in front of her and her two friends. The officer's expression spoke to anyone in attendance their visit to the Pentagon might take a sudden U-turn.

And his comment, through clinched teeth, verified it. "Ladies, put the camera away. It's against the law to take pictures of the Pentagon."

~~~

Ben had to curb the urge to laugh when his wife and Rosie tried to stuff their cameras into any pocket of their pants. But Rosie's comment made him switch gears and pray for a speedy intervention from the Lord.

"Sir, I'm noticing you're suffering from a tad bit of agitation, but I for one didn't see any of those signs you're talking about."

The officer's shiny bald head, face, and down to his collar shot from flesh tone to reddish/pink in mere seconds and he seemed to struggle with the ability to form politically-correct words.

Ben watched him take a deep breath. And with more calm than he probably felt since he'd stopped to discuss matters, he stated, "Ma'am, there are SIGNS posted everywhere. They tell you the taking of photographs is illegal."

Before another sassy retort came out of Rosie's mouth, Ben took the reins. "Sir, signage here in DC is confusing." He proceeded to tell him about them passing the same building multiple times on their way to the Pentagon.

"I agree. There are days I get lost coming to work." The officer laughed.

Ben thought they'd almost finished their discussion, but then he remembered he had a question for the officer about their parking spot. "Sir, is it okay to park here to go see the memorial?" He gestured to his truck.

"No. You need to follow the signs to the shopping center. Go under the overpass and turn on Red, White and Blue Boulevard...

The policeman lost him after the street named for the colors of the American flag. Ben wanted to tell him, "All we want to do is see the landmark. Please don't make me find, or follow, any more signs."

He waited for the man to finish his directions, and then thanked him. The Early Birds walked to the truck and as they got situated inside Jeff announced, "I don't know about the rest of you, but I think it's time to move on. We'll see this one another day."

A symphony of "Amens" reverberated from the front and back seats of the truck. Ben agreed and started his vehicle. "Jeff or Mary, since you're our travel guides, what's next on our agenda."

"I'll get directions for the Lincoln Memorial and it looks like there's three parking lots next to it. We can see the other memorials too."

"Great idea, and I'm telling every last one of you - if I ever resorted to drinking the hard stuff, I'd think about it today. I saw my life flash in front of my eyes when we almost got thrown into the slammer, and it was none too pretty."

Ben stayed put for a good five minutes after Rosie's comment. When he started to take off, someone said something else, and he had to put his vehicle back in Park.

While he dried his tears, Ben thought of the likelihood of Rose tipping a bottle of anything alcoholic. The possibility rated right up there with jumping out of an airplane. No way. No how. Not on their friend's bucket list.

When Ben settled down and pulled his truck out of the Pentagon's parking lot, he had to give his friend trouble about her comment. "I know you'll never imbibe, but if you decide to, let Bets know. She's our new videographer and will film you."

"Benjamin Stevenson, you'll do well to get us out of here before the cop changes his mind. And, stop the talk about me wanting to guzzle a particular beverage. The only spirit I want inside of me is the Holy Spirit."

Once more laughter filled the dually and Ben smiled at his friend. He agreed with her. No need to have alcohol to calm the nerves. But having two cops vying for their attention at the same time—that made for way too much excitement in one day.

Tomorrow, Lord, can we get back to our agenda of helping humanity? Sightseeing takes too much work.

CHAPTER FOURTEEN

"I don't know about anybody else in this truck, but a visit to the ladies' room is next on my list. Mr. Lincoln will have to wait." Betsy hit the back of Ben's seat, hoping he'd get the drift and park. ASAP.

"Hon, I'll find a place to park here as soon as I can, but this dually doesn't fit in typical spots."

"Like on the beach in Florida."

"Rose, be quiet about water. Ben, if you stop, I can get out—"

Ben pulled over and Betsy, Rose, and Mary exited the truck and headed up the knoll to the memorial. About halfway up, Bets stopped walking. "Mary, do you know where we're going?"

"No, but moving gets us closer to ask someone where the restrooms are."

"I think I see a ranger next to the water fountain."

"Rosie, if you mention water again, I'm going to lock the door and not let you in the room, if and when we find it."

"Need I remind you your sense of humor goes down the toilet when you…never mind. Oh, there's an arrow pointing to the ladies' room.'"

"And it's closed for cleaning."

"I think it's only the men's room, Bets."

Betsy opened the door and walked over to one of the stalls. She pulled the door towards her and almost fell backwards when she saw a little girl sitting on the stool. Tears streamed down her cheeks.

"Honey, oh my goodness. I'm sorry I walked in on you." Betsy opened the door to leave, thinking the child's mom must be in the next stall.

"I was hiding, but no one's come to get me." The child wiped her face with the hem of her shirt.

"Betsy, are you talking to yourself again? And why are you talking like a kid?"

"For once I'm not chatting with myself, but when you get done, you might want to come over here. I have something, or someone, to show you."

She helped the child off of her perch and together they walked out of the stall. An audible gasp met them and Betsy wanted to take a picture of her two friends. They stood with their mouths wide open.

"She surprised me too, and we need to find her parents." Betsy knelt down. "Hon, what's your name?"

"Kelsey Sue O'Brien."

"Hello, Kelsey. My name is Rose. How about you let go of Betsy's hand and come over here for a minute?"

The youngster did and Rosie moved her head and displayed the strangest hand movements in Betsy's direction. It took a minute, and then she realized what her friend meant and did what they came in to do.

Once the foursome finished, they searched around the building for the girl's parents. Betsy surmised, if anyone appeared frantic, they'd be the ones. Everyone looked normal. All except the man on stilts. *Another strange thing to write about.*

They headed down the hill and out of curiosity Betsy asked the little girl, "Kelsey, why were you in the restroom all by yourself?"

"My brother pulled my hair. It hurt and I hided from him."

"Brothers do that." Mary came over and smoothed the little girl's curls. "But in this big city, it's better if you stick closer to your family."

"My friend is right." Betsy grabbed Kelsey's hand and they started to walk to the ranger station she'd spotted on their sprint to the facility. As they neared a picnic table, Bets overheard a woman, "She's only seven years old—"

"Mommy. Daddy." Kelsey dropped Betsy's hand and rushed over to them.

The man swept the girl into his arms and hugged her. "Kelsey, thank goodness you're okay. Where did you find her?"

"In the restroom at the top of the hill. And Kelsey gave me quite a start when I found her."

"I'd say Betsy almost—"

"Never mind, Rosie. He doesn't need all the details. Anyway, your little one is safe and sound. That's what is important"

"And, it constitutes a hug."

Betsy gave Rosie a moment with the mom then attempted to set the captive free. "Rose, let the poor woman go. She's been through enough today. No need to smother her."

The smile on the mother's face said she'd welcome

more hugs, wherever and whoever they came from.

"Oh, and by the way, we're the Early Birds and you have no idea how happy I am that I had to use the restroom today."

"Don't let her fool you. She's the only reason we ever stop our RVs. This time, Betsy, your bladder saved the day and if you didn't notice, we've accomplished another Haphazardly Handing out Hospitality."

"Whatever you call it, thank you for finding my daughter." The man took out his wallet. "Can we give you money for lunch?"

"Please keep it. Glad we showed up when we did." Bets cleared her throat. "And, Kelsey, promise me the next time your brother pulls your hair, give him a big kiss. You'll never have to worry about him doing it again."

"Yuck. That's gross."

Betsy leaned down and whispered for only Kelsey to hear. "Miss Mary over there told me she did it to her brother and he never yanked her hair again."

"I'll do it then." Kelsey giggled.

Betsy straightened up, but before she moved too far, the little girl gave her a hug. "Thanks for helping me find my parents."

"Our pleasure, sweetie. Now we have to scoot to find our hubbies or they'll think we got lost."

"Don't have to look too far, we're behind you. I see you've made a new friend."

Betsy spun around when she heard Ben's voice and proceeded to tell him, Larry and Jeff about their adventure. "And, I'm certain Kelsey won't be venturing off again."

"Nope. I'm staying right here." Kelsey smiled as

she held her daddy's hand.

"That's my girl." Betsy headed up the hill again. About halfway, she stopped to check on her friends and hubby. Ben and Larry lagged behind. "Are we going to see this memorial today, or not?"

"After I use the ladies room again."

"Mary, you had to say the word, I'm right behind you. Betsy?"

"Me, three."

~~~

As they navigated the stairs to the Lincoln Memorial, Ben held Betsy's hand. People of every make and model milled around the enormous marble statue. While they strolled among the crowd, he read the words etched on the walls and decided he'd taken a history lesson for the day.

Most of the visitors spoke in hushed voices. Almost as if they stood on sacred ground. In Ben's mind this one held an importance, but the next memorial they'd see—the Viet Nam Memorial, topped his list of places he wanted to visit.

Ben missed the draft by two or three years, and when he graduated from high school, and then college, a career beckoned louder than the military. He'd always wondered what his life would have been like if he'd joined.

"Are you sleeping over here?" Betsy jabbed him in the ribs.

Oh, I'd have missed marrying the love of my life.

"With the grin you're wearing, I'm afraid to ask what you're thinking."

"I'm imagining my life without you and it wasn't pretty." Ben put his arm around his wife.

"That's good. You were scaring me. Thought you were plotting ways to get rid of me."

"Never. You're a published author now. I'm waiting for the big bucks to roll in from all the sales."

"Don't hold your breath, or you might be the one dying. Just a reminder, I'm not published. We'll wait and see."

Ben collected the unsuitable thoughts racing through his head. No need to say them out loud. When he did find more beneficial words, he said, "Hon, neither of us is going anywhere, except to the next memorial. But, FYI, you need to reread your verses in Philippians."

Betsy's furrowed brow, and then her wide-eyed recollection of what he just announced made him laugh.

"Oh my goodness, Ben, haven't thought of them in a while."

She then took out her phone. A second later, Ben heard the voice on Google as it recited the verses in Philippians. Then Betsy proclaimed, "I'm a changed woman now that the Lord and my hubby reminded me of my foibles."

"Happy to help."

"Bets, what is Benjamin doing? Is he helping you with the title of your next book?" Rose snorted as she approached them. "I still say mine is a keeper: *Crazy Birds On the Road...Again.*

"I'll write it down. Again. Along with everything else I've seen today. About Ben, he was actually jogging my memory about the verses I better reread."

"Over, and over and over—"

"Mr. Stevenson, if you're done with your Bible teaching, are you ready to head to our next stop?"

"I am." Ben grabbed Betsy's hand and they hiked the short distance to the Vietnam Veteran's Memorial. As they neared the black granite wall, humor faded and any words he wanted to say caught in his throat.

Lord, may we never forget their service and sacrifice.

CHAPTER FIFTEEN

Tears streamed down Betsy's face as she stood next to the wall. As a writer, her mind ventured to the soldiers' untold stories. Still so much for them to share, but their lives ended too soon. *Forever young. Forever heroes. Forever in our hearts.*

"I hate to interrupt you, dear, but if we want to miss rush hour?"

Ben's voice surprised Betsy and she babbled something, which she hoped sounded like "I'm ready."

"Not sure what you said, but the others are waiting for us on the lawn."

No one said a word on the way to the truck. Not even Rosie. Their red eyes told Betsy the memorial touched them as it had her. But less than ten miles into their trip, Bets heard a snicker coming from the other side of the back seat.

"Are you going to tell us what you're laughing about?" Jeff questioned his wife.

"It's obvious from what I'm about to say I've spent way too much time with the Birdettes. Our time in Colorado taught me so much. And, what's going on in my mind, you might not find as funny as I do."

"Try us, I've heard we laugh at the stupidest things. Don't we, Rose?"

"Hush up, Betsy. Go on, Mary."

"After we located Kelsey's parents, the title of Betsy's book came to mind. I wanted to tell them, 'Bets has a new book. It's a comedy called *Always Enjoy the Journey*. And it's sure to help you over the trauma of your daughter going missing in a toilet. Oh, I mean bathroom."

Betsy tried not to laugh, but the absurdity of her friend's statement made it impossible not to. When the Early Birds merriment lulled, she said to her friend, "Mary, I need a marketing person and it looks like you're my first employee."

"What about me? I thought I was your CEO of Marketing and Daily Operations."

"Ben, you and Mary can fight over who does what. And from what I see from my author friends in Houston—marketing takes a lot of time and energy. I'll need two of you to get things done."

"The Early Birds will help…any way we can."

Rose's comment made Betsy smile, but part of it concerned her and she spoke before her brain kicked in. "If Mary came up with the idea she did, Rosebud, do I really want to know what your marketing strategies are?"

"Just you wait and see, missy."

"I have an idea. How about we market to funeral homes? Those people will be 'dying' to read your book."

"Lar, to go along with that one, we can promote Betsy's books at the RV Park in Florida. Remember the day the ambulance came into the park and Joe said, 'Rose, you do know we're in God's waiting room.' See there's more people 'dying' to read *Always Enjoy the Journey*."

"I'm 'dying' to have this conversation end and start talking about viable places to market my book. Or…are you telling me it's so bad only dead people want to read it?"

For the rest of the trip, everyone sang Betsy's praises. Two or three of them sounded as if they had the paperwork signed and ready to nominate her debut novel for the Nobel Peace Prize for Literature.

"Okay, enough already. For those who read my book, I'll take your compliments. Those who haven't, better read it before you throw out any more accolades. I'll think you're buttering me up for my famous potato salad. Can't be my fabulous writing."

"It is your fantastic writing, dear, and is anyone else hungry? Besides me? All this talk about marketing and food made me hungry. Do they have my—"

"As a matter of fact, there's one at the next corner."

"Thanks, Jeff."

"You're welcome, Larry."

~~~

Ben pulled into where they parked their RVs after their dinner and the afternoon of sightseeing, shenanigans, and servitude. He chuckled and decided they needed to make a bumper sticker with those three words on it. Plaster it on their RVs.

He got out of his truck and heard a few muffled "fun day" as his friends headed to their campers. But tiredness left as soon as Patrick announced. "If anyone's hungry, I've got a fire going. Marshmallows are waiting to be toasted."

"A man after my own heart." Ben unlocked their RV and brought Matilda out to enjoy the festivities.

"Ben, did you have Betsy text Patrick and tell him to do this? I saw your wife messing with her phone after we left Taco Bell."

"I did no such thing, Lar."

Patrick held up a hanger. "Ben and I talked about it before you left this morning."

"I always say, 'Plan ahead.'"

"No you don't dear, but how about we go and get some S'Mores? I'm famished."

Ben followed his wife and as they rounded the corner, he admired the spread Patrick set in front of the fire. It rivaled any he'd seen at the countless bed and breakfasts they'd stayed at over the years.

Comfy chairs. A roaring fire. Bottled water and sodas in a cooler on the picnic table. Hospitality surrounded them and Ben added a note to his phone. *Give A+ review on the boondocking site.*

Patrick took a chair and moved it closer to the fire. He loaded his hanger with four marshmallows and Ben watched as he twirled it over the flame. The younger fellow pulled them off the fire and blew on the blackened treat. "Who wants the first batch?"

"Ben," Every voice rang out at the same time and Rose chimed in with a snort or two.

"They know me too well."

"Then here you go." Patrick piled the marshmallows on a graham cracker and handed it to Ben, along with a chocolate bar. While he loaded his hanger again, he asked, "What did you see today in the big city?"

Ben enjoyed hearing his friends talking over each other. He let them chit chat since the gooey dessert captured his full attention. For the most part. That was until Rosie brought up his wife's bathroom habit.

"Patrick, I don't want to say she visits every facility we go by, but we're topping out at ninety-eight percent."

"Rosie, I don't believe our host wants to hear this part of our eventful day. Cut to the good part."

"Had to set the stage."

"No, you didn't. Patrick, how are those marshmallows coming?"

"They're burnt."

"See, Betsy, what did I tell you? My storytelling had him enthralled. He couldn't move his hanger 'cause he was afraid he'd miss a part."

"Ignore her, and give me the charred ones. No need to throw them away. I'm learning to love them burnt."

He constructed the same sweet sandwich and handed it to Betsy. She devoured a large bite, but kept staring at Rosie. Ben never had a doubt she chowed down on the plentiful portion to keep from stuffing it in her friend's mouth.

The one still fabricating stories. Ben gazed in awe at Rose's recollections of their day's events.

"The little one was one step from dehydration when we found her. Poor darling. And, I saw a person lurking outside the bathroom when we came out."

Rose's version of the story caused the Early Birds to lose it. Ben watched his wife and determined once again, if S'Mores didn't inhabit her mouth, words a plenty might occupy the evening breezes.

Then he saw the hint of a smile on Betsy's face and

Ben knew something entertaining dawdled on his wife's tongue. Also, Larry handed Bets a napkin and she wiped the corners of her mouth. He must have sensed a spectacular finish to their evening in the fields of Virginee too.

Betsy raised up a bit in her chair. "Rosie, if an evil person prowled outside the restroom we were in, they'd see you and run far, far away. You'd scare him clear to…what's the farthest point in the United States?"

"Alaska."

"On this coast, Mary."

"Northern Maine.

"Thank you, Larry. And may I add. Rose, you are nuts and so is your storytelling. Mary, you'd agree with my assessment?"

"On which part?"

"That our friend is a looney bin."

Mary raised her hand and squeaked out, "Yes, she is."

"Patrick, the true story is we found Kelsey in the restroom. Thankfully we located her parents a short time later and all ended well. No boogie man snuck around outside for any of it. Except, maybe, the man on stilts."

"I like my version better. More intrigue and a happy ending."

"Rosebud, my suggestion is for you to write down your take on our adventures. Betsy's next book needs more implausible scenarios."

"Funny and farfetched are the perfect pair."

"And it explains everything. Larry, I'll bring over my manuscript Rose edited. She wanted me to go down a rabbit trail where my characters solved mysteries in the next two towns they visited. Need I tell anyone - I don't write mysteries."

"I'm trying to help you sell books."

"I appreciate your assistance, but it's still not what the publishing house I contacted expects. Especially after I told them I write Christian Comedy."

"Add, 'Christian Comedy with a Twist', and you can—"

"I don't need to add anything. Remember, I'm sending the full manuscript to Mr. Pickle tonight. Not changing anything."

"I hope he tells you to put in a little zig."

"He won't." To put an exclamation point on their conversation, Betsy waltzed over and messed up Rose's hair, and then she came back and took her chair.

Ben loved watching Rose and Betsy's lively exchanges. No worry in the world, or neither wondered if those who had only met them considered it strange how they interacted with each other. Two women in their own little world. And the one woman, he loved with all his heart.

~~~

"Patrick, if I was you, I'd think twice about letting us stay after this display of idiocy." Betsy smiled at their host.

"You're welcome to stay as long as you want. I haven't had this much fun since college."

"Enough about us. How about you tell us your story and all about this spread we're staying on?" Betsy settled back into her seat.

"It's a long story, but a homeless man I met in Washington, DC changed my life. Most of this property belongs to him. Mr. Bill Channey."

"Don't want to point out the obvious, but how does a fellow living on the streets own acreage in Virginia?"

"Normally they don't, Jeff, but you have to hear the whole story to understand."

"Get going, Patrick. The Early Birds love a good story."

"And this is a good one, Rose. My friend, Colby, and I are in downtown DC and this man is standing near a building, holding a sign. Didn't have much money on me, but something, or Someone, prompted me to give the man the couple bucks I had."

"Rose Wilford knows all about giving to people standing on street corners." Betsy snickered and she heard the others around her do the same. Patrick gawked at them and not to keep their new friend wondering, Betsy said, "We'll tell you about it when you finish."

"Can't wait."

"Yes, you can, but it'll be hard to beat. Go on now."

Patrick shifted in his chair. "Don't know Rose's story, but I think mine will top it. Corey and I stayed and talked to Bill. He shared stories about his wife and his years in the service. Sad part was when he got to his son. They'd lost touch and he didn't know his mom had died."

"The last part of your story beats mine."

"I'm not done. Just getting to the best part. Corey asked Bill if he wanted to eat dinner with us. He did and over a cheeseburger and fries, Bill stole our hearts and changed our life's paths."

"Sorry to interrupt, but does anyone want a water?" Ben walked over to the cooler. "Got any popcorn? This movie's getting interesting."

"And the sooner you sit back down; the sooner Patrick will fill us in." Rose motioned to his chair.

"Continue."

"After dinner, we asked Bill to stay with us at the hotel. Don't think any of us got any sleep. Or the next two nights. Every day we'd get up after a few hours and head out. We didn't figure it out until later, but Bill stopped panhandling while he took us around DC."

"Hope you got to see the memorial at the Pentagon. Our visit there didn't work out so well."

"Betsy, we did see it. Plus, some we'd never thought to check out. Along with having Bill as our tour guide, Corey and I continued to ask him questions. We found out the last place his son lived and I called my dad. He contacted a friend and he tracked down Bill's son, Barry.

"When we let Bill know, he asked if we'd stay for their reunion. Neither of us wanted to miss it. Funny, his son only lived an hour away in Leesburg, Virginia. That weekend, Barry and Bill connected and the four of us talked into the wee hours. Not a dry eye in the house."

"I love this story and since I'm a writer - I love happy endings."

"Betsy, here's your happy ending. The next morning Bill brought us out here. We found out he wasn't homeless and he had Barry, Colby, and me pick out the acreage we wanted. After a dollar for each acre passed between us, he filed the paperwork and we were land owners."

"You own how many acres?"

"Give or take fifteen, Larry. I butt up to the acreage Corey took. When his fence falls down, like it is now, I claim it." Patrick laughed.

"You gave a man money and you find out he's not homeless."

"Like I said, Ben, he had a sign. I assumed it'd say what they all say. 'Need work...'" Patrick's face flushed.

"What did it say?" Betsy swiped the front of her phone to write down what he said. Especially after his faced glowed a handsome shade of red.

"God loves you. Ask me about Him."

"Patrick forgot an important part of the story."

"Hi, Bill. Early Birds, let me introduce you to Mr. Bill Channey." Patrick sprang from his chair and gave the old man a hug. "Okay, what did I forget in my story?"

"The part where I don't give my property to just anyone walking the streets. But when they showed Christ's love the way these two did. They took me in and fed me. Enough said. Nice meeting you."

"There you have it." Patrick dabbed at his eyes with his shirt sleeve. "I think you'd agree it was the best money I've ever spent. Ben, if you don't mind, can you stoke the fire? We need another round of S'Mores. I'm ready to hear more about the Early Birds."

"Our stories might convince you to leave here and hit the road."

"What I've heard about your travels today, Larry, I'm ready to go shopping for my own RV. Come and meet up with your caravan when you're touring the East Coast again."

"We'd all love to have you."

CHAPTER SIXTEEN

Again Betsy saw Mary wiggle in her chair after Larry's *all of them* comment. Were the Miller's planning on going somewhere without them? Another mystery to solve. And she'd get Rosie involved to stop their nonsensical thinking of leaving the group.

Maybe Betsy imagined her friend's jiggling in her seat. Maybe Mary suffered from...*heavens no I'm not going there. Maybe I need to ask her and get to the bottom of it.* "No pun intended."

"Patrick, don't worry about Betsy. We lose her at least twice in a lengthy conversation. Normally she cracks herself up and by the time she tells us what's gone through her head, we're rolling on the ground too. Bets, you want to share your latest with us?"

Betsy squirmed in her own chair as she tried to fabricate a tale. Inspiration leapt forth and out of her mouth, "As a writer, I have an excuse to zone out. Don't mean any disrespect. Sometimes the usage of my time is better spent inside my head."

"Baloney sandwich with a slab of cheddar cheese. Hold the mayo." Rose ended with a loud grunt, not her usual snort.

"What?" Betsy stalled for time.

"There's no 'what' about it. I can almost see the gears churning inside your head. It's the same look you had when you badgered me about where I'd been. Don't know what you thought I was doing, but I'll bet you had me robbing a bank."

Too perfect. Take the focus off of me. Thank You, Jesus!

"Well?"

"No, Rosie, we found out you were out buying cantaloupe...coupons...that is."

Betsy listened as her friend recapped her faux pas and she still couldn't believe Rosie visited the questionable place then gave the man the coupons from it. Writers only hope to come up with a scene with such richness and naiveté.

Lucky for her, she traveled with the one who'd mastered it. Betsy smiled, knowing the cantaloupe caper would appear in her next book. Her concern— would she be able to pull off the humor? She'd give it a go.

Betsy heard uncontrolled laughter from around the fire pit and knew Rose reached the end of her narrative. She decided the time had come to call it a night. "I'm going inside. Need to send an email."

"I'm right behind you, dear."

Betsy took Matilda for a short walk around their spot then trudged up the steps to her computer. She opened her manuscript and sighed. Another glaring mistake. "Hon, sightseeing is out for me tomorrow. It'll be a late night for me to get this to Mr. Pickle."

"After hearing Patrick's story, maybe it'll be a good

day to help him and Corey with the fence. Helping others, one post hole at a time." Ben took out his phone. "I'll text Larry and Jeff. See what they think."

Betsy heard her hubby's comment, but instead of saying anything in return she stared at the manuscript on her computer screen. Once again she slipped into her own little world. Oblivious to anything going on around her. Ben and his texting included.

Until someone banged on the side of their trailer and Matilda's barking brought Betsy almost out of her seat. Ben hurried to the door and held their dog as he opened it. "What's going on?"

"If you've never witnessed a birth of a miniature donkey. Pixie's ready. Right now." Patrick's gloved hand pointed in the direction of the barn.

"I'm game. Let's go."

Betsy put on her tennis shoes and they followed Patrick, along with the other Early Birds, to the barn. One look at the attire told her their host roused them from slumber. No comment for now, since birthing a miniature donkey took preference over someone wearing moose pajamas.

And she intended to chat with Rosie about her husband's choice of sleepwear after the big event. Larry usually stuck with the NFL or MLB attire, not wild animal prints, and she wanted to know who bought him the wildlife pajamas.

"The show's about to begin."

Patrick's voice took Betsy away from her friend's fashion failure and directed it to the end of an animal she never thought she'd pay attention to. But there they stood, facing the backside, and the mama tried everything but standing on her head to help the baby out.

The wee one struggled to enter the world. Head first. Not sure which direction Betsy fathomed for a normal entry for a baby donkey, and since she hadn't given birth herself, she watched the proceedings with wonderment.

The front hooves followed the head, but then it seemed the babe got stuck. Patrick stroked Pixie's side and talked to her in a whispered tone. Betsy supposed he did it to keep her calm.

The baby made a sudden move and its mother let out a dreadful sound. Colby ran in from the side of the barn and took hold of Pixie. Patrick pulled the baby and after a few tugs, it came out. He then placed the newborn on the straw and the mom started to clean her up.

Without turning to the audience, he said, "it's a jenny. A girl, for those who don't speak donkey."

Betsy teared up when the mama tenderly nuzzled her baby between licks. The 'jenny' stretched out her legs, acting as if she'd woken from a long winter's nap.

Rose rushed over and hugged Betsy. "We haven't done anything, but I feel like I've given birth and I want to send out announcements."

"Girl, you go right ahead. I'm going home and write this in my journal. Another possible scene for my next book." *Book?* Bets stopped talking when she remembered what she'd left behind. *And I need to go to the RV and get busy on it.*

"Hey, let's leave Patrick alone and go to bed." Ben walked out of the barn and stopped next to Betsy. "Hon, I recognize your I-need-to-edit look, but it's already 11:30. It's time to snooze. Tomorrow you can tackle it with a fresh perspective."

"And, a better attitude. In general."

"Amen to that," Mary and Rose echoed the words as they walked arm in arm.

"You two don't even know what Ben and I are talking about." Betsy poked Mary this time.

"Do too. Ben enlightened Larry of your glaring boo boo. I blabbed it to Mary and Jeff."

"It's nothing a skilled writer like myself can't fix. Whip. Whoop. Wing. A masterpiece is reborn."

"We've seen one birth tonight. Don't need to see another. Say Goodnight, Betsy." Rose came and gave her a hug. "And night all to everyone else. Come on, Larry, bring your mooses and let's go home."

When calm returned to the pasture, Betsy said, "Rose Wilford, I hope one day we'll go a whole twenty-four hours without you making an off-the-wall comment."

"It'll be the day of Christ's triumphant return from heaven. I have my speech planned out and the videos I want to see of my life, but I'm certain I'll think of something else to say contrary to what I've written down."

A snort led Betsy and Ben to their door. When Bets reached their bottom step, she swung around. "You do know we can't tuck a piece of paper into our clothing when we're laid to rest, don't you?"

"With technology, at the rate it's going, God will have a fax machine up to heaven before it's all said and done."

Mary's laughter rang out the loudest in the darkness. While Betsy tried to discontinue her own chuckles, she thanked the Lord Jeff and Mary found the expansive property to camp on. And if she and her friends didn't nip something in the bud soon, they'd wake the new born.

"You do know when we find her funny, we're encouraging the crazy woman. Who, at the moment, is standing next to a grown man wearing animal-print pjs—"

"Whose designs on his pajamas he will never live down. Like other topics—i.e. trying to avoid light poles. Rosebud, it's bedtime." Larry took his wife's arm and pushed her up the one step then gave the Early Birds a backward wave.

"She leaves herself wide open and then wonders why we laugh. I do love Rosie Wilford."

"I'm going to mis—"

"Mary, you are going to do what?" Betsy directed her full-on radar at her friend.

"I'm going to bed. Yep. That's what I'm doing."

Betsy wanted to do more than poke her this time, but instead of chasing after Mary, she chose her own bed. In less than a minute she lounged between the sheets and drifted off into dreams of perfecting her manuscript.

Duplicate words. Oh me. Oh my. Lord, quiet my beating heart.

CHAPTER SEVENTEEN

The next morning, Ben hauled himself out of bed and dressed as quiet as the small square footage allowed. Witnessing the birth of a donkey made for a short night and Betsy needed sleep before she fine-tuned her manuscript.

His knowledge of all the rules of writing might fill a small thimble, but Ben knew one thing – he LOVED how *Always Enjoy the Journey* turned out. *And I need to compliment my wife more often.*

Ben went over to Betsy's desk and wrote her a note, telling her not to change too much in the process of checking it over. "Make the corrections you need to, but it's almost perfect, sweetie. Don't change too much. ☺"

He put the pen down and returned to the kitchen to pour his morning cup of java. Another thought hit him. Her discussion the other day about 'finding your voice'. As far as he knew, she'd found hers and he didn't want her to lose any of it. "She's a one of a kind writer."

"Glad you finally figured it out."

Betsy's voice behind him caught him by surprise

and he almost threw his drink in the sink. "Next time, dear, make a noise. You were in the direct path to receive a cup of very hot coffee."

"While you're over there, want to fix me some?"

Ben filled his wife's twenty ouncer and brought it over to her desk. "Don't want you to have to get up."

"Appreciate it. And what is this?" Betsy held the paper he'd jotted the note on.

"A love note."

"Sweet. I promise I won't change anything to just change it. I'll pray about them first."

"I hope so." Ben leaned over and kissed her. "I'll be praying for you while we're hard at work on the fence."

"Will you do me another favor. Pay attention to Jeff. See if you notice anything about his behavior."

"Hon, are you taking Rose's advice and switching from comedy to suspense writing?"

"Heaven's no."

"Then why am I paying attention to Jeff?"

"Remember when I said Mary was acting like she had ants in her pants. She did it again last night. *Then,* she said, "I'm going to mis..." She left the sentence unfinished, Ben, and tears sprang to her eyes. "I can only imagine what she was going to say."

"So you want me to lie in wait for Jeff to do an oddity and this will help you figure out Mary. Got it."

"When you put it that way, no, but watch him without him knowing it."

"If I'm looking at a guy for more than three seconds, I'll figure they'll have their phone in their hands calling a psychiatrist. Betsy, men don't stare at other men to try and observe what they're up to. We ask, "hey, dude, why is your wife acting like her shorts are on fire?"

Betsy smiled and reached over and touched her hubby's hand. "Hon, with Jeff, you might want to be a little subtler in your questioning."

Ben laughed then saw a slight frown forming on his wife's face. "Okay, I'll put on my investigator's cap and see if anything stands out. Now get busy. Love ya. Come on, Matilda, time to repair some fencing."

~~~

Like I know how to fix a farm fence. Ben mumbled the words to himself on his way down the stairs. *I've nailed boards, but...*

"If you think any harder, your head's going to explode." Larry closed his outside compartment and flung the tool belt over his shoulder.

"Ever done a fence before?"

"Living in Texas you learn lots of different skills. It's been years since I've worked on one, but I'll take it's like riding a bike. Get on and go."

Ben retrieved his own belt and strolled over to Jeff's RV. He raised his hand to knock and the door opened. Their friend exited his rig and if anyone took in his facial features, they'd say he'd sucked on a lime and didn't enjoy it.

Not wanting to comment on his observation, Ben remained quiet. Patrick finally came over. "We can all fit in my truck."

"In your dreams." Jeff leaned over and straightened the crease in his jeans. "These legs don't fold. I'll hop in the back."

"It'll be bumpy."

"Even better. Could help my mood."

Ben noted the interchange between the two men and

he began to feel sorry for the nails Jeff would pound in the fence, when they started work. Whatever happened in the Miller household, fur flew and feelings—from his past experiences with Betsy—took time to mend.

Even though he'd poo pooed his wife's earlier request to check out their friend, Ben decided he'd pay closer attention to Jeff. Ask him offhanded questions while they fixed the fences. Maybe he'd help him restore order in his friend's home.

And I'll text Bets too. Have her see if she can get anything out of Mary?

Despite the numerous pot holes on their journey out to the fence line, Ben wrote the note. Errors and all. He wanted to send it with the misspelled words, but he'd never hear the end of his bad textmanship.

Ben grinned as he corrected his mistakes then sent the text at the same time Patrick stopped his truck. Jeff jumped off the back and came up to Ben's side and leaned in. "Want to tell us why you're all chipper this morning."

"This is the day—"

"Yeah, I know. It's the day the Lord did something, let's rejoice and be happy about it."

"Jeffrey, you've been memorizing verses. Wink. Wink. I'm so proud of you." Ben almost caught a smile before it disappeared.

"I prefer Jeff, if you don't mind, and can't someone have a sour disposition once in a while? I deserve it."

This time, when the scowl appeared on his friend's face, Ben didn't know if he wanted to run or ask more questions. But Larry and Patrick, moving towards them, made his decision. Wait for another time to talk.

"While you two were jawing over here, we secured

three posts. You two get to do the barbed wire. Patrick said you'll need these." Larry handed Jeff and him a sturdy pair of leather work gloves.

"What will you be doing?" Jeff put his on and wiggled his fingers.

"Don't mind him, Lar, Mary woke up Grumpy this morning and gave him to us for the day." Ben chuckled.

"I can say Betsy sent Happy along to keep us entertained. How about we go to work and my mood might improve?"

"Sounds like a plan, but I have to ask Patrick how Pixie and her baby are this morning?"

"Slept out with the pair and they're doing great."

"Good to know. Now can we get going?"

Ben followed his cranky friend across the meadow. Next thing he knew, Jeff stopped and he ran into the back of him. The bigger man spun around, with his hands raised, and Ben thought he'd meet the hereafter before his next breath.

"Don't worry, Mr. Cheerier-Than-I-Can-Stand. You're safe. I'm not going to pommel you in the ground like the fence post, but leave me alone. Your...our day will go much better if you do."

Whatever burr wedged itself under Jeff's saddle, Ben would leave it be. No need to rile a grizzly bear out of his den unless you had to. He'd pray for his friend and decided to not pick on him as much.

For the next hour and a half, Ben learned valuable lessons about barbed wire and the damage it inflicted on parts of the body left uncovered. One wound required a bandage. Once he secured it with duct tape, and buttoned his shirt sleeve, he joined the other men.

"How about we take a break? Ben looks like he's

about had it." Patrick came over with four waters.

"I've worked hard on other jobs, but this one hurt more. Drywall doesn't talk back." Ben unbuttoned his sleeve and showed them the nicks on his arm he'd left unbandaged.

"Ouch. The wire got me too, but not as bad." Jeff lifted his shirt and red marks covered his side.

"Other than us showing each other our wounds, like in *Lethal Weapon,* we'll live. One good thing, Bets will be glad I wore this shirt today. She's threatened to throw it away the next time it was in the laundry. I'll save her the trouble. I'll take it off and put it in my rag bag."

"Without washing it. Remind me to steer clear of your underneath compartment."

"Which reminds me, Jeff, did I ever tell you about Larry hiding his casino gaming device in Betsy and my compartment?"

"Don't believe you did, but the story sounds interesting." Jeff smiled.

Ben started the story about Rosie finding Larry's iPad, but didn't get too far before his friend piped up, "He has it all wrong, Jeff. I wasn't hiding it, the gadget fit better in one of Ben's plastic containers."

"When we get back to the RVs, I'm asking Rose her version. It'll be closer to the truth." Jeff threw his crushed water bottle in Larry's direction.

"I'll pay for your lot fee for the next two nights, if you don't." Larry tossed it and the bottle hit Jeff on the side of his head. The misguided projectile caused everyone in the crowd to crack up.

"Larry, you're aware Patrick is not charging us rent? Boondocking is free."

"How true, Ben, and...to give you all a heads up – Betsy, Mary, and Rose are heading over the hill."

"They are and they better be bringing snacks and/or something to drink other than water."

"Soda's not good for you on a hot day, Larry. Hydrate."

"Thank you, Dr. Stevenson. Another MD in our midst, along with Rosie, will cause my blood pressure to go haywire. Anyway, from the grins our wives are wearing and lack of a picnic basket, their visit isn't about eating. No, wait, Bets has a backpack on. We're in luck."

"I don't doubt they've brought us lunch, but the three of them did something and we're going to hear about it." Jeff gave a nod in their direction.

"Lord in heaven, please don't let it be another piece of property. I already own a building in Ft. Myers and don't want another one."

"Larry, I'll sell you acreage in Colorado for a cheap price. It's waterfront. Thanks to a flood a few years ago."

"No, but if Rose has a new venture, my taillights are the last thing you'll see on my way to your property. Get me away from the wacky woman I'm married to." Hysterical laughter overtook Larry. He teetered and before anyone caught him, he dropped down to the ground.

"Larry Wilford, if you're not having some kind of attack, get up from there. Us ladies have news for you, Ben, and Jeff. Especially the latter."

CHAPTER EIGHTEEN

Rose's voice echoed across the expansive field. Even the cows in the adjoining field perked up when Betsy's friend announced their arrival. And the news they had to share—quite a doozer, if she said so herself.

"Boys, oh I mean men, gather round. We have an idea and it's going to knock your work boots right off your feet."

"Rose, as much as I appreciate you sharing the concept we came up with, I might need to talk to Jeff about the proposal first. Get his take on it. Let's eat the sandwiches we made and we'll chat about other things."

"Mary, what's going on?" Jeff came up next to his wife.

"It's actually a brilliant idea and solves almost everything we've been talking about."

"Go on, Mary. I can't wait to hear it."

"Folks, since you're having a meeting, I'm out of here. We can finish the fence tomorrow." Patrick walked to his truck and drove away.

"Okay, Mary, let's hear it."

"Jeff, we've been putting off telling our friends about the possibility of us going back to Colorado. Today, when Rose said something about our visit to Jenny, what we've talked about spilled out. The truth is, telling it to them helped solve our problem."

"Which is?"

"The piece of property we want to sell. Instead of selling it, why can't we go back and turn it into an RV Park? Colorado needs more of them and the land is in the perfect location. We'd also be near Jennifer so I can help with her wedding plans."

Betsy wished they'd brought chairs since Jeff appeared to need one. Thankfully the new fence held him when he leaned against it. Also, his brow wrinkled as if his wife spoke to him in a different language.

When Jeff finally spoke, it had nothing to do with their land. "Mary, I'm confused as to why you're discussing our problems. Thought Betsy had work to do on her book. What in the world does our wanting to sell our land have to do with…what's it called that Bets is doing?"

"Editing."

"Thanks, Betsy. I ask again, what does—"

"Betsy finished and came over to the RV. Mary was already there. We're chatting, like we do. Next thing I know, Jeff, your wife erupted like Old Faithful on its daily schedule when I asked her, "Are you planning to go back to Colorado to help Jennifer with her wedding?""

"And her reaction cemented my suspicions. I've been watching Mary. I figured she either had something to tell us, or I was going to suggest she go see a proctologist. Too much fidgeting going on."

"Jeff, ignore Betsy, but think about the possibilities, dear. This will give us a place to put our RV in the summer and still give us the ability to travel to Florida in the winter. To spend time with the Early Birds."

Rose's arm shot into the air and a snort came out of her that almost brought all of them to their knees. Betsy swung around and saw her friend as she too took a seat on the pasture. Her tears, a series of wails, and more gibberish than at the Tower of Babel, flooded out of her.

"Hon, I'd suggest you get up before a snake bites a part of your anatomy you'd prefer it didn't. Here let me help you." Larry reached out a hand and his wife leaned her head on her propped-up knees.

"Dear, I don't know what brought this reaction, but whatever it is, it can't be that bad."

"It's worse." Rose lifted her head and dried her tears. "When we talked, guess I thought they'd do the RV Park and run it like we do Sassy Seconds *Two*. Own it, and then find a manager so they'd still be able to play with us. All twelve months."

"If we do this, we'll still be around to 'play' with you. It'll only be part time." Mary chuckled then said, "I don't know, but this conversation sounds like we're in junior high. Not in our late 50s and 60s."

Another sob escaped from Rose, but after a minute she quieted down. Might have had something to do with the cows. They'd stopped eating and came over to the fence and stared in their direction.

Betsy extended her hand to Rose this time. "With the knowledge I have of bovines, I'm convinced they'll stay put. But just in case, let's move this party to the north forty, wherever it is. Come on. Get up little lady."

Rose took Betsy's hand and stood, wiping at her eyes again. "This means the Early Birds are breaking up. We won't be the six chums going around this great land of ours - haphazardly helping humanity." She smiled. "I'll miss you."

"We'll miss you too, but we haven't done anything yet." Jeff moved to stand next to Rose. "I do like your idea though."

"Whatever you're going to do, don't forget to pray about it. It's how a solid foundation is built."

"Even if it means we break up the team, Rosie?"

"Even then, Jeff. I don't like any part of it, but if this is where the Lord leads—I'm all for it. Who knows, after you open the RV Park, we might come and work along with you two extra-special people."

"Don't want to repeat myself, but aren't we getting the cart before the horse."

"Mary, most of the ideas we think of materialize. Like Mr. Pickle said, "hold onto your hat". The Lord's about to fling some gates open and we better get ourselves ready to walk through them."

"I say again, how does my wife toddle to where we're working, announce a grand plan for someone else, and then crumples to the ground when she hears the ins and outs of it. Then she ends up praising her heavenly Father for what He's about to do in their lives."

"Larry, you're married to her. I'm doing all I can to figure out Betsy."

"I'm with you on this one. I mean about Mary. Dear, I do ask—next time, please consult me first. Not positive you'll find this comical, but the thought of an RV Park hit me yesterday. Yes, I think the Lord is about to do something. We better keep watch."

"And pray, pray, pray."

"Amen, Sista Rose."

~~~

"In Jesus name. Amen," Ben closed out their morning prayer and he took a bite of his cereal. The thought of Jeff and Mary leaving, or even thinking about it, weighed heavy on his mind and Betsy's sniffles told him her side of the story too.

"I wanted to know why Mary squirmed, but I can't believe Rosie and I helped them make the decision to part ways."

"Hon, you or Rose aren't responsible. Sounds like they've been thinking of going back to Colorado for a while now. Maybe they planned to make it a short visit, to sell the land, but once they got there, they'd have stayed."

"The ladies and my visit there in May to see Jennifer almost made me want to stick around longer than two weeks. Those mountains lured me in. Even after all the years we spent in Texas, my heart is still attached to Colorado."

"I get it and it's why you wrote about your favorite place. Speaking of *Always Enjoy the Journey*, how did the skimming through it go this morning?" Ben finished his breakfast and put his bowl in the sink. "Come over here and tell me all about it."

For the next ten minutes, Betsy gave him the play-by-play analysis. While she recapped her trip of going back over her book, Ben realized he hadn't read the latest. Only those in the beginning. "Can I read your book? See what you've done since the last time I set eyes on it?"

"Why not."

He read while Betsy peeled potatoes for another batch of potato salad and straightened up their RV. The little bit of noise his wife made, puttering around, didn't bother him. Her words flowed on the screen and he smiled, laughed and kept scrolling through the pages.

"Benjamin, you haven't said a word in over an hour and a half. You hate my book or you're coming down with the flu." Betsy touched his forehead. "Temperature seems normal."

"I'm fine, and this version is fantastic. Don't know how you improved on the one I read before, but you did." Ben stood and took Betsy in his arms. "Hon, I've said it before, and I'll say it again. I'm sorry for all the hassles I gave you about your writing years ago."

"What? Harassment? You? I don't remember. Kiss me you fool."

They kissed and Matilda joined in with howls loud enough to wake their fellow campers. Ben picked up their pooch and pretended to include her in their smooching session. Their dog lasted only a minute in Ben's arms then jumped onto the loveseat.

"I don't know when that started with her, but I get a kick out of it every time." Betsy reached over and patted Matilda's head. "Just so you know, Miss Princess, jealousy will get you nowhere. Now, if you two don't mind, I need to go finish making everyone's fav-or-ite dish."

Ben lounged next to Matilda while Betsy chopped the cooked potatoes into cubes. Instead of his usual scrolling through Facebook, today he chose to gaze at his wife while she worked in the kitchen.

Her wrinkled brow caught his attention. She'd

obviously not found as much humor in the memory he'd mentioned and stood chewing on it. This caused Ben to get up from the loveseat and fetch Matilda's leash. A walk around the property sounded good to him.

"Going somewhere?" Betsy dried her hands on the towel she'd grabbed off the counter and stepped in front of their door.

Oh, Lord, save me from the impending doom that's about to strike.

CHAPTER NINETEEN

Betsy stood at the door and wanted to laugh out loud at her hubby. She imagined his differing expressions conveyed a litany of decisions going on in his head. *Do I run as fast as I can from conflict? Or, do I stay put and act like nothing's wrong?*

She stepped away to see which direction he'd choose. Ben, with Matilda, opted to flee the 'danger' he imaged inside their RV. Even if he thought she wanted to scalp him for talking about their past offenses, truth be told—her frown at the sink came from overcooking the spuds.

"Sorry, Lord, for not stopping Ben from running for his life, but he is a kick to watch. And while he's gone I'll recheck the potatoes. Maybe I can salvage them." Betsy snuck a gander into the yellow bowl and forked a couple. "They're keepers."

Betsy finished her task and put the bowl in the fridge. And no more putting off her next job. "It's time to send the manuscript to Mr. Pickle." She checked it over one more time, and then hit Enter.

When the email disappeared, Bets gave a

triumphant, "that's a wrap" and proceeded to check her Sent file. There it sat and now the publishing house had it. With Ben's endorsement and her own stamp of approval, they agreed *Always Enjoy the Journey* sang a comical tune.

Or at least Betsy hoped it did. She'd cracked herself up and the others who'd read it, including Mr. Pickle. Hadn't he said his side hurt after certain scenes? But Betsy's biggest questions—would they publish her book? And would anyone buy it? She hoped so, but...

"If they do publish it, Ben and I will be brainstorming ideas for marketing."

"What am I doing?" Ben and Matilda wandered in the door and her husband wore a smile, telling her he heard her proclamation.

"Put on your corporate cap and help me with marketing ideas. Events we can attend to promote my book, when *or* if it published."

"Funny you'd mention events. I checked a deal in Pennsylvania. An RV show. It's not until the end of next month, so it will give us plenty of time to get copies of the book, business cards, and whatever else you can think of."

"Oh brilliant CEO of mine, where are we having the supposed books shipped?"

"Great question."

Betsy laughed at Ben's not-thought-that-far-ahead-look and decided she'd save his brain from exploding. "How about we wait for news from Mr. Pickle then you can find an RV Park in Pennsylvania and we'll stay put for a while."

"Splendid idea and I'll find a place we can fish at."

"You don't fish, dear."

"But Larry does. Jeff too. They can teach me everything they know."

"Scary thought, but Mary and Jeff may already be on their way to Colorado." Saying it made Betsy want to turn the clock back to when she and Rose suggested the absurd plan.

"You're beating yourself up again, aren't you?"

"Yep. And I will until they change their mind—"

"Betsy, your plan only happened yesterday. As far as I'm concerned, they'll weigh the pros and cons of owning an RV Park and one or both of them will sprint as fast as they can to a realtor and sell the property."

"Hope you're right."

"I'm always right."

"Keep believing that, my love, and since you're in such a good mood, I have something funny to tell you about our earlier conversation." Bets took the bowl from the fridge. "Since you scampered out the door so fast, you missed the real reason for my supposed sour disposition."

"You weren't mad at me?"

"Nope. I thought I'd cooked the taters too long. I was bummed I'd have to start over with another batch."

Ben wore a sheepish grin and said, "Next time I won't assume you're angry. I'll save bolting from the scene for when you turn crazy on me. I'd give you an example, but I can't think of one."

"If that amount of foolishness hasn't already occurred, taking Rose and my actions at times, you've been sleeping. But if the book is finally published – I'm not counting on any kind of sanity. I know we will be the blind leading the blind down the dark alley into the abyss—"

"Hon, your last statement proves you're a writer. And together we'll figure it out."

"Promise me you won't take flight when I need you. Your clear thinking will come in handy if things start getting out of hand, and I'm not talking about me here. Only the circumstances surrounding marketing."

"Sure you are, sweetie."

~~~

Time at Patrick's flew by faster than staples into the fence post. Ben thanked the Lord when he plugged the staple gun into the generator. It made their mending job go so much quicker. In the ten days they'd spent helping their newest friend, the Early Birds had repaired all things broken.

Ten days and one visit to Washington, DC. Oops. Maybe more trips on their way back down. Ben pondered this development over a turkey bacon and egg sandwich Betsy surprised him with for breakfast.

"Hello. Anyone home?"

"Come in, Rosie."

"How'd you know it was me?" Their friend's voice rang out. As she hit their threshold she announced why she visited them at 9:00 in the morning. "The men can add fence mender to their resume. Patrick said we're free to fly."

"Are those his exact words?" Ben glanced over at her and she stuck her tongue out at him.

"I'll ignore your backtalk. And the open road is before us once again. How about the Early Birds talk about our next stop when we meet later? Larry's giving me a refresher course in driving the big rig. Got a little rusty since I haven't done it since Ft. Myers."

"Rosebud, you do know what you're standing in is a

big rig. Not the one you own anymore." Larry sauntered up the steps and stuck his head around the door.

"It's all in how you perceive it, Lar. When I'm driving, even out here in the open field, I envision our RV is five to ten feet longer than its actual length. So when I'm on the road and I want to pass someone, I'll not wipe their front end off when I pull back in."

"That I'm grateful for. And today, Rose, I'll be teaching you from my manual: Mr. Wilford's RVing 202 – The Use of Mirrors.'"

"Is this the lesson you teach which keeps the student from running into light poles?" Ben's laughter filled their RV.

"If you were closer, Ben, you'd have heard the word 'mirror'. The class I teach on utility-pole avoidance will be at a later date."

"Aaron, at the driving school, suggested I swing wide when I approach a pole, unlike another person in the room. But when I'm passing a car, I'm to check the mirrors as I go by them. When I see their full vehicle in my side mirror, I'm safe to pull into the right lane again."

"I'm happy Aaron gave you those pointers. How about we get your driving lesson done? I've got things to do to get ready to leave in the morning."

"Okay, let's go and I'll show you how it's done."

"You'll show me something."

"We're leaving?"

Larry lagged behind. "Patrick did say we were finished with the fence and said to tell everyone goodbye. He had to leave early to run into DC for the next two days."

"Maybe Bill's around and I can leave him a bowl of potato salad I'm making. I'd think you guys were sick of it two weeks in a row." Betsy lifted the spoon as if any of them wondered what she stirred together in the large bowl on the counter.

"You're not giving any of it to anybody. It's ours."

"Mr. Stevenson, our mission is to help humanity. Sharing goes hand in hand with what we're doing in our travels."

"Thank you, Miss Humanitarian, but speak for yourself. My journey includes eating the proceeds of what my wife makes. Since we all know her cooking abilities are very limited, and I mean VERY limited, I need to take advantage of them when she hits a high note."

Ben reached over the counter, into the drawer, and took out a fork. However, his attempt to scoop out a taste came to an end when Betsy hit the end of the utensil her hubby had brought out.

Betsy, and those in attendance, watched it as it flipped into the air. When it landed on the tile, it made quite the clatter. No one said anything as Bets picked it up. And their stares told her they waited for her to tell them the punch line to a joke she'd started and hadn't finished.

She remained silent and Ben, Rose, and Larry inched toward the door to leave. To quicken their departure, Betsy tossed the fork she'd picked up into the sink and said, "Ben, I'll text Rose when your departure from this earth isn't so imminent. Then you can come home."

~~~

Ben and his friends raced down the RV stairs and

once they reached the picnic table and sat down, he said, "We're safe."

"For the time being. Benjamin Stevenson, you're in so much hot water it's clear up to the thinning hair on the top of your pointy little head."

"Rosie, there's no need to remind Ben of the sticky situation he got himself into. And, since we've wasted so much time discussing side dishes, I'm going to pull the RV back to our spot. No more driving lessons today."

Ben watched Larry walk in the direction of the field where he'd parked their RV. Rose headed after him, but he didn't let her get too far and asked, "Have you gotten a text yet?"

"Nope. Haven't heard a buzz. You do know she's put the potato salad away and is planning how to take you out and not end up in jail?"

"I'd say I wasn't the brightest bulb in the string of lights a little while ago, was I?"

"Don't stew about it. Bets will get over it. You'll live to see another day."

"I hope so, but to stay safe, I'm coming over to your RV and help Larry. Bets doesn't want me near ours."

"I'll let you know when I get her text. Knowing Bets, she'll send one within the hour. While I wait for it, I'm going in to see what's to eat. That's after Larry brings our RV back over."

Their scenario played out in front of Ben. Rose walked to their assigned RV spot and even though Larry had it under control and moved to the area with ease, she kept her arms raised as he approached.

They started to flap around until Larry honked and stuck his head out of the RV window. "Rosebud, if you don't move out of the way, you'll be able to roast marshmallows on the exhaust in about a minute."

"As of right now, you old poop, your end date is looking like today too." Rose moved over and one last arm movement took her inside their newly-parked Class C.

Ben strolled over and helped his friend as he prepped for the Early Birds departure in the morning. While Larry rolled up their outside rug, Ben unlocked the grill/fire pit and carried it to his side compartment. He opened it to set it inside and Lar yelled, "S'Mores later?"

"Good idea. Guess my mind's preoccupied with my wife's diabolical plan aimed at me. Rose is probably on the phone and they're scheming together right now."

"Betsy, or Rose, isn't going to take either of us out. But I do recommend you consider what you say about your wife's cooking next time. She might quit making it and I don't want to miss out on several large helpings of my favorite dish. Thank you very much."

"Still can't believe I said it."

"I can. Done it myself, as you saw a moment ago. But it won't be the last time we say something idiotic. Another suggestion, which I failed to follow today, don't have people around when you mess up. Seems to go better when you don't." Larry laughed.

"How about we go in and smooth out the rough waters called our life." This time Ben chuckled. "Anyway, we can finish all this tomorrow."

"Thought you had to wait for Betsy's text?"

"Don't have to. Your wife waved at us a minute ago. I'm heading home."

"Hope the 'all clear' goes for me too?"

Ben moved toward his trailer. "Lar, it's all good. And I'm not talking about Betsy's potato salad this time. I'll bring you some for dessert. You'd rather have it than the sweets any day."

"Yes, sir. Oh, and you might want to bring Jeff a bowl too." Larry looked around. "Where are those two? I'll go check on them right now."

"Lar, you're stalling."

"How can you tell?"

CHAPTER TWENTY

"Ben's backside isn't telling me much, but he's dragging his feet on his way to you. BTW: Larry's toast too."

Betsy put her phone on the counter after reading Rosie's play-by-play text of Ben's forthcoming arrival. She tried everything to nix the laughter bubbling up inside her, but hilarity won the fight.

When Ben strolled in, she tried to stifle her giggles. But his expression which said, 'I've come back to a peaceable situation', almost ruined her attempt. In reality he hadn't, but Rosie's comedic text put Betsy in a better mood for them to discuss her hubby's prior penalty.

Or not. As Betsy sprang into action to chat with her other half, her phone buzzed. Multiple times. Only one person they knew sent numerous transmissions and her name began with 'R'.

"Rose is on a tear. She's tempting us with S'Mores. Better answer her or she'll—"

"Here. How about I solve this?" Ben gave her a smile, which made her heart do a dozen jumping jacks.

A back flip occurred when she read his return text.

"Can't, we're busy smooching. Leave us alone. ☺" Ben placed her phone on the counter and took her hand. "Let's go sit on the loveseat so I can explain myself."

They did and Betsy put the foot rest up. "Never hurts to be comfortable while we discuss the world's problems. And if you're wondering, I'm feeling special. I'm more important than dessert."

"Don't test me on Taco Bell. On a good day, I'd pick you over a—"

"Never mind. You blew it." Betsy grinned this time so her hubby knew he hadn't stepped on her toes again.

"I've been doing a lot of that today."

"Can't be perfect all the time."

"I'm nowhere near perfection, but I'm ashamed to say I did what I've told you to quit doing over the years. Negative voices aren't good coming from you, and especially not when I say them to you. I'm sorry, Bets."

"Ben, I had an epiphany after you left. Don't know if the plain yogurt had anything to do with it when I added it to the potato salad, but that's when the profound thought popped into my head."

Betsy waited to let her words sink in and they must have hit the bullseye. The grown man she adored appeared to almost lose consciousness when he realized what she'd said.

His babbling alerted her she'd better clear it up. ASAP. "Honey, I'm joking. The potato salad is fine. Just wanted to get your heart racing."

"It worked. I'm still a little delirious. How about we have a helping of your deliciousness? It'll make me feel better, while you tell me the revelation you had."

Betsy doled out two generous helpings of the side dish and handed one to Ben and said, "Enjoy."

The bite her hubby took measured less than a sliver. And watching him eat it made her think he still thought she'd done something to it. *Really?* Betsy solved his tentativeness by taking a generous spoonful and eating every last stitch of it, licking the spoon for every morsel.

Ben's utensil flew into his bowl and he soon devoured the helping of potato salad. With his mouth full, he asked for more. Betsy obliged and he finished it too. "Hon, you've outdone yourself this time."

"Yeah, right. I'm remembering someone an hour ago—"

"Your not-so-bright husband is so sorry and wants to know what he can do for his wife to make it better?" Ben carried his bowl to the sink and squirted soap into it. "Here, let me wash the dishes."

"That's a start. Just so you know, you're still in hot water."

"I am. Literally." Ben held up the dishrag.

"Cute." Betsy took it and cleaned the area around the sink and bar area where Ben splattered most of the water then said, "Unlike me, at least you're a great cook, but you are a messy cleaner-upper."

"I am and proud of it." Ben took the towel off the stove and dried his hands. "Now, what's next, my dear."

"I think I'd like to talk."

"Matilda, I'll count to three and we'll escape from here together. Are you ready to go outside?" Ben's words created chaos in their pooch and she headed straight to their door.

"Benjamin Stevenson, you know when you say o.u.t.s.i.d.e., Matilda understands what you're saying. Now you need to take her for a walk to do her business, but don't think of stopping to get a S'Mores on your way back home."

"Never crossed my mind." Ben took the leash off the hook and fastened it on their dog, even though Matilda continued doing her dance. As they walked down the stairs, Betsy heard him tell her, "Mats, you make this so difficult."

Ben reached the last step and Bets leaned out and whispered, "Don't forget to bring me one too."

Less than five minutes later Ben appeared at the door with Matilda and two S'Mores on a paper plate. Betsy hoped her hubby gave their pooch an opportunity to do everything she needed to do. If not, she'd alert them later to get it done.

"Eat 'em while they're hot." Ben handed her the dessert when he came back in. "They're looking good."

Betsy gobbled hers down, and decided instead of sitting inside and discussing the same old thing they'd chatted about dozens of other times, she wanted to go outside. Pull up a chair next to the fire and fix another goodie.

"Bets, I know what you're thinking, but we're not going out there. Let's have our talk." Ben's hand shot to his mouth then he removed it and said, "I didn't just say—"

"You did and we do need to clear up some unfinished business."

Ben undid Matilda's leash and took the seat across from Betsy at their table. She tried to formulate her words, but decided instead of dilly-dallying about the correct way to say it, she'd just blurt them out, "Writing is giving me an attitude and I'm thinking of giving it up."

~~~

Betsy's announcement almost caused Ben to fall out of his chair, but he stayed upright. They'd battled for years about the writing topic. And without a hint, she dropped this bomb on him. *Help me, Lord Jesus. F.A.S.T.*

"Hon, I don't know why you're not saying anything. You can't tell me you haven't noticed my attitude. Another issue—my procrastination is at an all-time high. About my writing, it's…Ben, will you say something?"

Ben continued to pray while he did what his father did when posed with a problem. He rubbed his forehead. Then the perfect words came to him. "I thought the reason for your attitude had to do with me. Good to know I'm safe."

He wanted to add a tad more, but she swatted his arm. "When I want you to take something serious—you always make a joke. Or, vice versa. Ben, if I didn't love you so much, I'd…"

"You'd…what? Let me think. You'd give me a kiss. Right here." Ben pointed at his lips as he leaned across the table. "And, another thing, dear, I want to stay one step ahead of you. How about the kiss I mentioned then you can tell me more about your attitude problem?"

Betsy gave him a smacker sure to wake him up then she retook her seat. "Benjamin, you're not fooling me. I've witnessed a miracle from God Himself. He gave you the words to say. Those didn't come from you." Betsy whacked his arm a second time.

"I cannot tell a lie. Me and the Lord had a quick chat. I love when He answers as quick as He did today."

"Saved you from sleeping at either of our friend's RVs tonight."

"Then I'd miss conversating with my honey. That one came from the Lord too. I'm on a roll this evening."

"You're on something. Anyway, Ben, back to what I said, which caused you undo stress. I don't want to per say give up writing, but letting people read about us—wrapped in a fiction package, I don't know."

"Bets, I'd stay mad at my earlier comment about your potato salad, before I'd worry about any of that. Trust me, they will not sit in their chair and say, "This is too real. I must put it down." Ben tried to contain his laughter, but lost the battle.

"Laugh all you want, mister, while I suffer through these feelings of inadequacy. If Mr. Pickle walked in this very minute, I'd tackle him to get my manuscript back. Ben, it needs more work. I know it does."

"It doesn't need anything. Leave it in their hands and they'll decide what your book needs. Until then, leave Mr. Pickle alone and start your next book."

"With this attitude? As we've said for years, 'If your attitude doesn't change, you need to go to Attitude School. I'm signing up tomorrow.'"

"Just in case you don't want to go there, Rose is available for consultation on any subject you choose. She'll have you diagnosed in no time."

"I've already pinpointed my abnormalities. No need to bring her into it."

"I'd love to hear what she has to say about you

wanting to quit." Ben reached and took Betsy's hand, holding it so she wouldn't slap him for his next comment. "You are going to tell her 'cause if you don't, I will. This one is too good to pass on."

CHAPTER TWENTY-ONE

"Mary and Rosie, you're never going to believe what Betsy informed me of yesterday. She said she's going to quit writing and admitted she has an attitude," Ben hit the hood of his truck as he continued with his version of their story from the day before.

While he recapped her candor, Betsy sat in a lawn chair and propped her feet on the fire pit and listened. So much for his compassion on her situation showing through. Oh, she forgot. He's a man.

Not wanting the fabrication to go on any longer, Betsy hurried over to their truck. Her fist landed next to her hubby's and she said, "Ben's so full of potato salad, it's clouded his awareness of said situation. Listen to me, I'll tell you what actually happened."

"Wondered when you were coming over to quiet his nonsense. Bets, you aren't going to quit. Final. About the attitude, RVing cured your 'Stinkin' Thinkin', along with the verses you read. Whatever is true, whatever is noble, et cetera."

"Last time I checked, Rosie, et cetera is nowhere to be found in the Bible." Mary pulled her phone out and spoke into it. "See. There's lots of 'whatevers' floating around in the verse, but not one et cetera."

"Good one, Mary. And, for you Rose, I never thought I'd hear you quote the Bible and the great Zig Ziglar together, in the same sentence. Better jot it down for my next book in the series."

"What?" Ben chuckled and winked at his wife. "Not another one? Thought you were quitting."

"Mr. Stevenson, it's not possible for Betsy to give up writing. It flows in her veins, right alongside her blood."

"If I'm not mistaken, Rose, it's going through her brain, too. Almost every one of her thoughts connect back to writing. In one way or another."

"Blood flows up there, as well."

"Not sure you've noticed," Betsy nudged her husband. "But I'm standing here while you're having a conversation about me. Larry, come get your wife and put her to work. She and Ben are out of control."

"I'm busy. Jeff, can you help Betsy out?"

"No I can't, Lar, but Betsy, I have one thing to say on the matter of your writing, keep doing it. What I've read, I liked it."

"Now that we have Betsy and Ben's life figured out, we need to wrap this up and get on the road." Larry opened his side compartment and started singing *On the Road Again.* Betsy and the other Early Birds sang along, especially the part about 'friends'.

"I'll never tire of Willie's famous song, but the cows in the near pasture—I hope they suffer from tone deafness. We're so bad at harmonizing."

"Actually, Ben." Bill Channey smiled as he came from behind Jeff's RV. "I sort of enjoyed your group's rendering of the song."

"Sir, I don't know you well, but I'd get your ears checked if you liked what you just heard."

Betsy laughed at Ben's comment then walked over to the older man. "Please tell the cows to keep this to themselves. Don't want them telling Patrick about our songfest or he won't let us come back."

"I'm positive the cows won't say a thing. About you coming back, you're welcome anytime. The fence has never looked better and maybe next time we can get you to sing around the campfire."

"We're never singing in public again. At least I'm not." Ben folded up the chair Betsy handed him and stuck it in their underneath compartment.

"Be adventurous. And you've all heard the verse, 'Make a joyful noise unto the Lord'? I'd say this classifies. My suggestion to you, you better get going. Traffic won't improve the longer you wait."

"It won't matter, Mr. Channey. Today I'm driving on the backroads to who knows where. And if you're not aware, it's customary to hug everyone before the Early Birds leave. Hope it's okay with you?"

"Bring it on." The well over six-foot-tall man enveloped Rose in a hug. One which picked her up off her feet.

A moment later, Rose stepped away from Bill and it appeared she tried her best to catch her breath. When she accomplished it, she sputtered, "Quite an enfolding if I've ever seen one. Did y'all take notes on how it's done?"

"Bill, you've gone and spoiled her and you've brought out the Texas in our friend. Watch out, she's going to start fixin' or hankering to do something here any minute and we better brace ourselves."

"The only something I'm doing is driving and seeing we fulfill our newest mission statement with more flare than a sparkler on the Fourth of July. We've got more small snippets of the Savior's love to give out on our journey up the East Coast."

"Then let's get to doing it, Rosebud. I'd suggest you take your place behind the wheel so we can get this thing moving." Larry jumped into the passenger's seat and yelled out the window, "Thanks again, Bill, for everything. Especially the use of your property."

"My pleasure."

Betsy took her turn hugging Bill and the Early Birds left their first boondocking place. From the smile on Ben's face, they'd do it again. Amenities at a campground brought campers in, but the off-the-grid lifestyle, and the zero price tag, helped their bottom line.

"What are you thinking about over there? Are you plotting out *Always Enjoy the Journey – Book Two*."

"Nah, nothing so complex. Anyway, dear, I always invite you to those brainstorming parties I have."

"Good. Didn't want to miss out on any of them."

Ben's assessment of her expressions and aforementioned comment made her chuckle. But Betsy realized, when she carried on a conversation in her head, those times it appeared to all those around her, writing occupied her mind on a continuous basis.

I'm soooooo bad about that. Lord, help me to get better at curbing my obsession with the written word. Shut My Brain Off.

"Hon, you're doing it again."

"Breaker 21. Can you hear me?"

"Yes, Rosie, and all the truckers this side of Boston can too—"

"Wilford out. She can't chat. Say goodbye, Rose."

"Goodbye, Rose."

After they quit laughing at their friend's interchange, Betsy added, "Probably a good thing Lar took the mic. No telling what she'd do behind the wheel while talking. She scares the bejebbers out of me in a car. In the RV—Lord save everyone traveling near us today. Amen."

"Rose is doing fine for her first outing, but I agree with you. In her case, both hands ought to grip the steering wheel at all times and keep distractions to a minimum. Even on backroads."

"Unlike me. I'm a professional big-rig driver." Betsy tried to do a little dance in her seat, but ended up almost knocking Matilda off her perch with her elbow. "Sorry, buddy. Next time I won't use my arms."

"Hon, when you drive, you're hyper-focused. You've heard me tell you to loosen up your grip both times you've driven. Bets, if anything ever startled you, we'd be off the road and in the ditch before "I love you" came out of my lips."

"What a sweet thing to say, Mr. Stevenson. Hey, the next time I drive, how about we discuss ideas for Book #2, #3 and #4 while I circumvent the curves of the roads. See if we can plot perfection on public roads. Or, we can fine tune my novels while on the freeway."

Ben gave Betsy a quick glance. "Hon, I love helping you with your storylines, but is my input required? This morning is a prime example. Within minutes of leaving, I see your mind working. You're plotting a scene."

"It is required. You've given me great ideas. But this will tickle you. My thoughts when we left were centered solely on our boondocking experience."

"You weren't thinking about writing?"

"Not this time."

"What about the second time I caught you in deep thought?"

"Was writing all the way. But you'll be happy to know I've asked for divine intervention. Next time I'm obsessing over sentence structure, or creating a scene in my head, I've instructed the Lord to zap me and set me straight."

"This I want to see."

Ben laughed, but the absurdity of any part of their conversation pronounced to Betsy her passion for writing required more tweaking. Or her beloved might ship her to a writer's conference and tell her to stay put.

And if Bets let her hubby in on the random thoughts racing through her mind about her mom and Bill Channey, he'd leave her at their next stop.

CHAPTER TWENTY-TWO

"Breaker 21, there's a Walgreen's up the road, about two miles. The website says RVs are welcome. Baggies and water are on Mary's list."

"We'll wait for you. Unless Betsy's nee—"

"Matilda needs treats."

"Guess you answered the question, but now our dog is running around the cab of our truck," Ben added the last part as he followed Jeff's Class C into the parking lot. From the looks of the area, they had room for a fleet of semi-trucks and a dozen motorhomes.

After Betsy left with the other two ladies, Ben located a bag of goodies in the side pocket of his door for their pooch. The tiny, training morsels quieted Matilda down and she settled in her mom's seat.

"You realize you'll be moving as soon as your mama returns with your..." Ben almost blurted out the 'word' again, but caught himself. For good measure, he gave Matilda another teensy treat. "There you go, buddy."

Ben put the snacks away and studied a scene unfolding out of his windshield. He observed Jeff and

Larry, talking to a young man. They high fived each other. Then they hugged. One of those where you pat the person on the back a couple of times.

This is serious. Larry hugged the man and gave him money. Now they're praying.

Ben wanted to jump out of his truck and join them, but decided to sit tight. "I'm staying right here, Matilda. Don't want to disturb the Lord's work. They'll tell me about it later when we get parked—"

His conversation with himself stopped when he spied the women and as quick as his feet moved, he hightailed it over to them as they rounded the corner. His sole purpose—not to let them near their husbands, as they happily helped humanity.

"Ladies, how about we go get a treat of our own? But before we do, stay right here. Don't move. I'll be back." Ben ran over to Larry and threw him his keys. "When you're done here, put Matilda in the 5er and turn on the fan. Thanks."

Ben didn't wait for an answer and hurried back to his charges. "You three ready for—"

"What I'm ready for, Mr. Stevenson, is an explanation of why you accosted us right when we came out of the store. What's Lar doing? Did he run into another pole?"

"No, he didn't. RVs okeedokie. How about we go over here to *Swirls Galore*? Saw it when we pulled in. We can get some yogurt?"

"Rosie, I don't know what my hubby's hiding, but a dessert does sound good. Even if it's pretend ice cream."

"Great." Ben moved past them and took larger than normal steps to get to the shop. When he reached *Swirls*

Galore, he whipped around and the women still stood where he'd left them. They stared at him and all three had their hands on their hips.

Ben retraced his steps and Mary said, "Not positive what's 'great' about all this, but the sooner we go along with whatever Ben is doing, the sooner we find out what our fellows have done."

"Let's go." Betsy made a forward motion and the women headed in the direction of *Swirls Galore.* After they got their dishes of flavored yogurt and assorted toppings, the ladies took a table closest to the door.

Ben still had to get his own goodies, which included peanuts, chocolate chips and an extra drizzle of hot fudge syrup. He paid and walked over to the table. Betsy and their friends stared at him again. This time as he took his seat.

"Yep, he's keeping something from us. Never in all my days married to this man has he gotten peanuts as a garnish. It's always and forever walnuts. Fess up, mister, what did Jeff and/or Larry do?"

"We didn't do anything. It was all the Lord's doing. But heaven's rejoicing a little bit more today," Jeff said as he plucked an M&M off the top of Mary's yogurt.

"Get your own."

"I think I will. Come on, Lar, this might be the only dessert we get today."

While his friends fetched a bowl, Ben devoured his and determined his choice in nuts might become his go to the next time he visited a dessert shop. From the magnitude of Jeff and Larry's servings, when they came to the table, they'd chosen their favorites too.

They sat down and Ben asked, "Did you leave any for other customers coming in?"

"I did, but I needed nourishment after our bring-it-on-Jesus encounter this afternoon. Rosebud, I hate to tell you, but Jeff and I topped your coupon caper and no gift cards required. We're so on the Lord's list of getting it done."

"You do know it's not works that save us, but I must inform both of you—no one can beat the work of art I accomplished. Game on, Mr. Wilford, tell us what you two did, or have you decided to concede before you even begin?"

"Not a chance." Larry smiled. "Jeff, do you want the honor of telling them."

"It's all yours."

"Getting to the point is always a good thing too."

"Ben, I'm getting to it. Anyway, while I waited for Rose, I saw a man walk up to Jeff's RV. Not worried he couldn't handle it, but I decided to check it out. Wished I'd had my video camera. When Jeff got out, it was as if the young man had never seen anyone over six foot tall."

"I heard him gasp, Larry, then he asked us if we had a few bucks to spare."

"Early Birds, this is where the Lord stepped in, took my tongue, and moved it like it was a bow on an expensive violin.'"

"Quite the picture, and one I'll have in my head for a long while, Lar. I have to ask, are we going to get to a point soon, or do the ladies and I have time to get another round of yogurt?"

"Ben, you're sore 'cause you missed out. Sit still and we'll speed it up." Larry wiped his mouth with his napkin then said, "I told Brian, 'if you want us to give you money, we'll have to pray first.'"

"Old man, I cannot believe you said that." Rose scooted her chair closer to her husband. "You don't talk to us most of the time, let alone a person who comes up and asked you for money. Is your BP spiking again? Here, put your arms up."

"Rosie, leave me alone. I'm fine." Larry pushed his wife's hand away. "And, yes, I asked him to pray, which Brian agreed to. But it was his statement after we prayed. Almost made my knees buckle." He stopped and a tear slid down his cheek.

"Lar, I'll tell the rest, if you'd like?" Jeff moved his empty dish to the middle of the table.

"Go for it."

"After we gave Brian the money, he said, 'You didn't ask, but I'm using the money to get gas in my car. Then I'm picking up my mom and she's taking me to a rehab. Here's the card. You can write the number down and check on me later tonight.'"

"We said we trusted him and whatever he did with the money was between him and God now. Brian thanked us and left."

"Unbelievable, but as we've seen this so many other times. The Lord doesn't do anything ordinary. Look at the six of us."

"There are those who are more extraordinary than others." Rose reached over and stole Betsy's spoon and licked the last bite of yogurt off of it.

Ben watched the proceedings unfold in front of him and marveled at his wife's restraint, but it was short-lived. Betsy stretched across the table and nabbed Rose's bowl and, using her friend's spoon, she dove into it and ate the rest of it.

Betsy giggled as she placed her spoon next to the

empty bowl. "Have anything else to say, Rosie?"

"I don't about you snatching my yogurt right out of my hands, but Jeff and Larry's story is a winner. Bravo, gentlemen. We've tackled another Haphazardly Handing Out Hospitality and lived to tell about it. Betsy, on the other hand, she's on my short list."

"Might want to forego any plans to take Bets out. If we hurry, we can make it to the RV Park in Hershey, Pennsylvania and go on the tour at Hershey's Chocolate World before they close." Mary showed them her phone. "MapQuest says we're about an hour and a half away."

"Not wanting to address a topic none of us want to talk about, i.e. the elephant in the room, but if Mary and Jeff leave—who's doing our navigation? Who's going to plan our different trips?"

"Figuring out where we're going to stay is the only reason you want us around, Rose? Now we know where we stand."

"Oops. Sorry, Mary, didn't mean it to sound so harsh. I can blame it on Betsy. I've developed her way of wording things. Saying it before you think it all the way through."

"No, Rosie, you mastered that one years before we met. I learned it from you." Betsy slapped the table.

"Ladies, can we discuss this over chocolate? A whole mess of it is waiting for us and I can almost smell it." Jeff deposited his and Mary's dish in the trash.

Ben did the same then strolled over and put a ten in the tip jar next to the cash register. "This is for having to put up with us. We're a rowdy bunch."

The teenager behind the counter smiled. "Your table

is mild. Check out Friday night. The customers get a little wild in here."

In a yogurt shop?

Ben kept the inquiry to himself and noticed Larry and Jeff focused on their phones. He opened the door. "Who's leading the way this time?"

"I'll let Jeff. Maybe it'll convince them to stay with us. Not pursue an insane idea like a campground outside of Estes Park, Colorado."

"Or a second-hand store in Ft. Myers, Florida," Rosie said as she saddled in next to her husband.

"No reason to bring up our purchase. We're discussing Jeff and Mary."

"And since the *elephant* has come up in conversations two times in the last five minutes, how about we have an Early Birds meeting when we get to Hershey?"

"Splendid idea, Rosie, as long as we have it *after* our visit to the Hershey's Chocolate World. We can't discuss anything of importance without sugar."

"Of course we can't, Benjamin."

~~~

The sliding door of the Hershey's Chocolate World opened and Betsy's senses kicked into high gear. She envisioned an enormous amount of chocolate going into their tiny RV freezer. Ice? Who needed it anyway?

"I'm hoping heaven smells like this." Rose twirled around and Bets assumed she'd taken in the delicious aroma surrounding them and all control left her. One bad thing, while in mid-flight, her friend caused a tray an employee carried to totter.

The young woman regained control and held out the tray of goodies. "I get a lot of that around here."

"I bet you do." Betsy reached for a mini chocolate bar, unwrapped it and popped it into her mouth. "Yummy."

Larry came over to the worker. "You'll have to excuse my wife. She gets excitable around sweets."

"When they smell this wonderful, who can blame me?" Rose reached for a piece of candy. "Dear, I am sorry I about sent you and your candies across the room."

"You're not my first. I've learned to dodge arms flailing about a number of times."

"So you don't do it again, dear wife of mine, how about we go and get our tickets for the trolley?"

"Sir, the trolley doesn't leave for forty-five minutes. You'll have plenty of time to taste more samples before you head out. You can purchase tickets at the booth over in the corner. If you have any questions, my name is Kim."

Rose's eyes brightened. "After we purchase them, sweetie, can you direct us to where we can get the most bang for our buck? Don't want to miss a thing."

"Here's a map of the different displays inside the building." Kim smiled and reached behind a counter then handed them each a small bag filled with Kisses. "Enjoy the tour, and everything here at Hershey's Chocolate World."

Betsy peeked inside the bag. "Are these to tide us over?"

The young woman chuckled. "Don't want our patrons to go hungry on their travels."

"Hon, we never go without food for long. We're full-time RVers and we love to eat. All the time. Desserts top everything else. We also sing occasionally, but our version of *On the Road Again* leaves—"

"Leaves people stranded at the chocolate place and they are unable to catch the trolley on time."

"Alright already, Larry. Go get our tickets. Kim, we'll talk to you soon."

While the men bought tickets, Bets and the two ladies searched the candy store for what to buy on their way out. The scent continued to surround her and Betsy's credit card screamed from her fanny pack, "Buy everything. NOW. Chocolate will help you write more."

Her internal dialogue made her laugh and she started to share it with her friends when Ben yelled, "It's time to go."

For the next hour and a half, the driver and two college students entertained them with songs, and an occasional disappearing act. One of the young men somehow slipped out of the back of the trolley and appeared again as a different character.

He'd have changed his clothing, along with his accent. As a Brit, he waltzed up to Betsy and held out his hand. Not wanting to choke on the piece of caramel she'd put in her mouth, she grabbed a tissue out of her pocket and disposed of it. Then handed the used Kleenex to Rose.

"Are you serious?"

"I think you'd rather hold this than do the Heimlich on me. Or worse, have to give me mouth to mouth 'cause I've passed out."

"Ladies, can the man get on with his act?" Larry took the tissue.

The entertainer grabbed Betsy's hand and led her to the front of the trolley. "I've heard from one of your friends you like to sing a particular song. How many of you in the trolley know *On the Road Again*?"

Hands shot up, along with loud cheers. After the noise died down, the young man began to sing Willie's song. The people sang along and Bets mouthed the words she remembered, deciding next time she'd stash a copy of the lyrics in her pocket. In case it ever happened again.

There better not be a next time. If there is—Mary and Rose are coming with me.

CHAPTER TWENTY-THREE

"Hershey is going to have to make more Kisses since I ate most of them this afternoon. Especially on our jaunt around town." Ben undid another wrapper and tossed it in the air, catching it in his mouth with ease.

"Too bad the circus closed down. Benjamin, I'd drive miles to see your act." Rose snorted.

"See, Betsy, I told you I had a God-given gift and Rosie's my first adoring fan." Ben threw another candy up and had to move his head a smidge for it to land in his mouth. "No doubt about it. I'm good."

"Hon, as you disclosed to me years ago, 'keep your day job.' Oh, you don't have a job. Guess you'll have to keep driving me around in our albatross to pass the time away." Betsy squeezed Ben's arm.

"On that happy note, how about we head on back to the campground. If I'm not mistaken, we're supposed to have an Early Birds meeting. Is it too early for Jeff and Mary to tell us if they've made a decision to stay or go? What will it be?"

On the way to his truck, Ben saw the couple glance at each other. The grins meant one thing - they'd made a decision about Colorado. Not sure it was the news he or the others wanted to hear.

He drove to the RV Park and when the traffic cleared, Ben made the left turn into the park. He'd almost made it past one of the cabins when Jeff yelled from the back seat, "We've changed our minds. No campground for us and no need for a meeting tonight."

Ben brought his truck to a stop, after almost sideswiping the structure next to him and in a hushed tone said, "Jeffrey, after I park next to my RV, you better run and get into the confines of the one you own. There's a good chance I'm going to—"

"Hug them until we don't have a hug left in us," Rose interrupted Ben and a round of whoops and hollers erupted.

"Jeff, the next time you decide to give out big news. Don't do it when I'm driving. Okay."

"Okeedokie, but the reason I did it at such an inopportune moment—it's Mary's fault. She jabbed me in the ribs and the words came tumbling out of my mouth. No stopping them once they started."

"I have my doubts."

"I confess. I did it. The last jab he's talking about, I got a little too happy on it." Mary laughed.

"Glad you've decided to stay, but I am wondering how you made this decision so quick. I was teasing back there." Larry opened the passenger door and put his foot out.

"Lar, I don't know why your foot is hanging out of my truck, but if you bring it in and shut the door I can go and park. Let's meet outside, with chairs, in five minutes. Anyone late will miss the rest of the story."

Larry slammed the door and Ben zipped into the

driveway next to his RV. He let their pooch out and set up chairs for Betsy and him behind their truck. The others scampered over with their seats and everyone's attention zeroed in on Jeff and Mary.

"Today we're gathered in the sight of—"

"Jeff, this isn't a wedding ceremony. Quit kidding around and tell us what changed your mind," Ben asked the question as he kept his gaze on his friends. This time he saw Jeff poke his wife. The two giggled at their inside joke.

"The truth, Jeff."

"Rosie, the truth is, I don't want to clean toilets in a campground. Mary informed me she also refuses to do them. We even called our niece in Estes Park and asked her if she'd do it after she closed Penny Lane for the day."

"Jennifer assured me she and Peter would work in the office on the weekends, but that's where their helping hands ended. Can you believe it?"

"On top of their refusal to do restrooms, they said they're planning a wedding."

"Jeff, you weren't there, but we were in Estes Park when Peter proposed. And, that's why I'm not buying any of what you're telling us." Rosie smirked. "Anyway, Jenny and Peter's nuptials will take place long before you'd break ground on a campground."

"I'm with Rose, but *if* there's a bathroom situation, build them so all you have to do is use a high-powered washer to clean 'em. No need of gloves, or getting anywhere near the yucky stuff."

"Bets, what about getting the lights and vanity wet?"

"Have you not heard of HGTV? They recommend

pedestal sinks. You can get water all over them. About plugs on the walls and light fixtures, keep the spray of water down at knee level. No worries of getting zapped then.

"Oh, and one other hazard. Be careful of the toilet seat. A hefty spray coming from the hose might blow the flat projectile clean off the bowl."

Ben mastered architecture, but listening to Rose and Betsy's tips made him realized he needed to intervene before someone got electrocuted. "Jeff and Mary, if you're telling us the truth, the Early Birds will come to Colorado and clean whatever needs cleaning."

He watched Larry and Rose and they nodded. Betsy shook her head "yes" and added, "I hope you took notes of the overabundance of ideas Rose and I gave you. Labor saving and decorative all in one attractive package."

"Jeff, I don't know about you, but I think we've carried them on long enough?"

"I agree, and Mary, I do have to compliment you on your storytelling. It's improved since we hooked up with the Early Birds."

"Yours too, sweetie."

"Mr. Miller, you do remember a little while ago that I had the urge to chase you. The impulse has returned. How about one of you tell us what's going on. And it better not have anything to do with revamping a bathroom." Ben waited for another tall tale.

"Mary and I have talked about turning our property in Colorado into a campground. It's a big decision, but today changed our minds. Being out here on the road to pray for Brian and the ability to help Patrick and Bill is what we want to do."

"Jeff and I can't imagine not being part of the Early Birds. Ever. The six of us are a team."

Ben thought he'd better get out of his chair and grab the roll of paper towels before the ladies flooded the campsite. He handed each of them, men included, two sheets, then swiped at his eyes. *Pollen is bad this time of year.*

"We didn't mean to make everyone cry." Jeff stood and took more paper towels off the roll.

"You did. And I hope you're proud of yourselves for carrying on the way you did. But, Betsy, back to your high-powered washer idea. When we redesign the restroom at Sassy Seconds *Two,* I'm implementing your design. Wished I'd thought of it first."

"Ignore my wife's jabbering about bathroom redoes, and the answer is 'no' to renovations of any kind." Larry got out of his chair and folded it up. "Anybody else hungry. The yogurt, which I can't believe I ate, left me a while ago. I'm hungry."

"Oh my, we can't have that." Rose joined her hubby near their RV after she picked up her chair. She opened their underneath compartment and said, "Here, hon, give me yours. You're probably too weak to put it away. I'll do it for you."

"Rosebud, when the Lord made you—"

"He said, 'Glory be to all mankind, I've made someone almost as perfect as Me.'"

"I'm sure those were His exact words, and just so you know, He also knows I'm still hungry. Can someone feed me?"

Ben watched Rose as she dashed inside their RV. A minute later she came back with a flyer in her hand. "Larry, Izzy Italian is going to feed us tonight. All we have to do is call in our order and—"

"Give them a buzz and the guys will pick it up. Bets, I'll share a pizza with you. You choose." Ben headed to his truck. "Are you two coming?"

~~~

Ben clicked his seatbelt and backed out of Izzy's, after they picked up the food. The women came along—for no apparent reason—other than to make sure they brought every breadstick home with them.

And to get the men a handyman job at the restaurant the following day. Along with securing their employment, Betsy, Rose, and Mary found out the owner's sister owned a thrift store in the candy capital of Pennsylvania.

On their way to the RV, Ben listened to the lively conversation going on inside the cab of his truck. He'd gone only about a mile when he hit a pot hole. Square on. *Oh, that is not going to be good.*

A bank driveway looked the perfect place to stop and check for damage. Ben pulled in and parked then turned on the flashlight on his phone. The tires on the left appeared okay, but when he walked to the other side, and put the light down to check, the inside tire was flat.

The passenger window opened. "Ben, do you want me to call roadside assistance?"

"While you have them on the line, tell them to toss in a 265/75R16 tire. I'd rather have it in case the tire is ruined."

"Do we know where we are, Ben?"

He spoke into his phone and said, "Banks near me." In a flash, Google gave the name of the establishment and the address of where he stood. "Here, Lar."

"Hon, don't we have a spare?" Betsy stuck her head out the window Larry left the minute before.

"You do, but Benjamin Stevenson, I'm not up on Tires 101, but the one under here isn't going on this truck. It's squishy to the touch."

"Good to know. This goes along with the jack I left on Larry's workbench back in Houston, which is gathering dust. Anybody have good news to parlay? Love to hear some. Preferably helpful advice to get us on the road again."

"Love the pun and road-side assistance will be here in thirty to forty-five minutes. Hope we can microwave Izzy's when we make it home."

Jeff exited the truck and seemed to take his own sweet time surveying the situation. As he got up off his knees and brushed them off, he said, "I'm with Rosie, looks like both tires are flat."

"How many years of college did it take you to come to that conclusion?"

"Not too many."

"Didn't think so."

CHAPTER TWENTY-FOUR

Betsy lay in bed the next morning, contemplating the events of the night before. The man the company sent to help them aired up the tire, which got them back to the RV Park. But their other problem—it would take longer. No tires available for two more days.

She shot up in bed. "Ben, I've got it."

"What do you have?" Her hubby's voice came from downstairs.

"While you, Larry, and Jeff are waiting for tires, the ladies are going to visit Antonio's sister's shop. I texted Rose and Mary my excellent idea."

Ben appeared at their bedroom door with Matilda in his arms. "Hope one of them reminded you the men are working at Izzy's today. We're using Larry's car to get there. It's why I look the way I do."

Betsy chuckled. She hadn't noticed any difference in his attire, but kept it to herself. "No biggie, we can check her thrift store tomorrow. If I know Rosie, she called and woke them up and shared everything about Sassy Seconds *Two*."

"Hope the owner at Izzy's didn't give her a number

to do such a thing."

"I'm joking. Anyway, you three go ahead. I'll stay around here and check emails. Get on Facebook and—"

"Twitter and all the other social media things you're hooked up to. How about a blog? It's been a while."

"Those To Do lists only work when I glance at them." Bets hung her head. "I have a reminder on my calendar for two weeks ago. And last night I thought of the perfect one to do. Oops. I'm on it."

Betsy dressed and gave Ben a kiss on his way out the door. Next, she texted her two friends so they'd leave her to write. Her phone jiggled within seconds and both texted her the same message, "It's about time."

"Well then, I best get going on it." Betsy grabbed her coffee mug then took a seat at her desk and opened her laptop. Every fiber of her being wanted to check emails, but if she did—time always escaped her and she accomplished nothing.

Betsy got up and set the timer on their convection oven for two hours and strolled back to her desk. A half hour later, she'd written eleven words. "TWO WEIRD PEOPLE ARE MARRIED (and they live in an RV)."

The catchy title popped into her head after she sat down, but nothing else. "Matilda, help your mama. She's stumped on what to write." Bets imagined her pooch coming up with some tidbits about her and Ben. None she'd want to share with her email list.

"On the other hand, Mats, I'll figure it out." Betsy grabbed her Bible and opened the front cover. The verse she'd written years ago caught her attention. 'Do unto others as you would have them do unto you.'"

Betsy gazed at the words again. "Oh my goodness, Matthew 7:12, this should be the Early Birds verse. I don't know why we haven't thought of it before. This is what we do when we hand out blessings, we're always blessed in return."

Betsy put her fingers on the keyboard and typed a blog about their Haphazardly Helping Humanity on their travels so far that summer. When she finished, the title came to her: GOOD DEEDS.

She scrolled up and put it in and said, "Perfect." She also added a PS after her name: BOOK NEWS: Manuscript off to publisher – no news from them yet!

Betsy's fingers itched to add more to her postscript, but kept it simple and turned her attention to her emails. The one from Linnstrom-Peterson Publishing, with yesterday's date, brought on unsavory thoughts. But as soon as she clicked on it, her mood and attitude improved.

Dear Betsy:

I hope you're sitting down. The committee loves your book. Attached are the corrections our editors made on *Always Enjoy the Journey.* Please make the corrections and resend your manuscript.

The sooner we receive it the sooner we can get your book in print. Also, send me a list of areas you're visiting on the East Coast. We'll set up book signings. I'll be in touch with the information.

Betsy, if you haven't figured it out yet, your life has changed. Happy travels to you and the other Early

Birds. All of us at Linnstrom-Peterson hope you're working on Book #2. ☺

Mr. Andrew Pickle
Editor, Linnstrom-Peterson Publishing

Betsy squealed and Matilda jumped straight into her lap. "Mats, if I read you what this email said, you wouldn't believe me. I can't believe it myself. Guess it's a hold-onto-your-hat kind of day."

Her phone buzzed and she read the text from Rose. "Are you staying in your RV all day?"

"No, Rosie, I'm heading over to give you and Mary hugs that's sure to shout to you my HUMONGOUS news." Betsy sent a shortened version of what she'd uttered and headed for the door. "Oh, I forgot. I better answer Mr. Pickle's email."

Betsy realized hilarity hit at the oddest moments. All her thoughts centered on - *how do you answer a pickle?* "Or in this case, Mr. Pickle? Do you send him 'sweet' nothings? Or 'bread and butter' blessings." More laughter ensued until Betsy gasped for air.

She contained her gaiety and patted the back of her office chair. "Matilda, come here. You need to write to him. I'm not getting it done." Their pooch strolled over, but instead of getting on the chair, she stayed next to her and tilted her head upward. "Mats, you're no help."

Betsy finally took a seat and penned an intelligent response. A 'woohoo' or two wanted to land on the page, but she kept a handle on her enthusiasm. Did Mr. Pickle know she wanted to hula all over happy? Yeppers, but she contained the zeal.

Ben? I have to text him. Betsy kept it low key, but hinted at her editor's news flash. Her hubby's reply redefined her earlier hysterics. "Headline: Pickle Provides Possible Provisions for Poet. Hon, 'writer' doesn't start with a 'p', so had to use an alternative. Congrats. Love ya."

This time she made it out the door and almost knocked Mary off the second step. "Next time I'll yell as I open the door."

"Not a bad idea. You want us to come in?"

"Please do. That way I can hug you then hop around like a mad woman in my own small abode." Betsy stepped away from the door and motioned her friends to enter.

"Well, girl, come and give me the best squeeze you got then tell us what's brewing. Other than coffee."

"Pour me one too." Mary sat on the loveseat.

After her friends took a seat, Betsy read the email from her editor and ended with telling them about Ben's use of the perfect alliteration. "He was having way too much fun with Mr. Pickle's name and what made it special—it didn't take him a minute to come up with it."

"Betsy. Betsy. Betsy. Honey, you've made us proud. And, as my hubby inquired, will you acknowledge us when stardom whisks you away from us? Ends up two of the Early Birds will fly the coop, leaving the others to fend for—"

"I've written a book, Rosie. I'm not starring in a movie. Just so you know, George Lucas is not going to come to any of the RV parks we're staying in and cast me in his newest *Star Wars* movie."

"You never know. If he does, I'll nominate Rose to play the stand-in for R2D2, since he's passed on and she's short."

Even through tears, Betsy saw a grown woman almost fall forward out of her loveseat from laughing so hard. Rosie caught her in time and saved them from making an emergency phone call to their husbands.

Decorum once again showed up, but Rose ruined it when she said, "I resemble that comment, but I can't play the part—I'm claustrophobic and get dizzy if I turn around too many times."

"This alone is why Jeff and I travel with you. You'd have to send us a video of the day's happenings, if we ever did leave and do something else."

Betsy and Rose stared at their friend and each tried to speak over the other, but Bets finally got the words out, "You're not changing your mind about going back to Colorado, are you?"

"No, but we still have the piece of property to sell. Hey, maybe we'll keep it and build a Sassy Seconds *Three* on it. Plenty of land to do whatever we'd want to do. Unless we…"

Betsy's merriment flew out the window with the words Mary spoke. Her friend's refusal to make eye contact and her unfinished sentence spoke volumes. *Lord, we're going backwards on this topic. Are they, or are they not staying. Help!*

"Since Bets is contemplating heaven only knows, I'll ask Mary. You're either selling or keeping it. Don't see any other choices. Do you?"

"I do and it involves Jenny's fiancé, Peter. Jeff and I had quite a long conversation with him about our property this morning."

"He's not going to build Jenny another house and studio, is he?"

"Rosie, a house isn't even the half of it."

"Do we need to keep guessing?" Betsy sat at her desk and crossed her legs. "Or are you going to tell us today?"

"I'm getting to it. You both know Peter's a builder. His plan is to build a large house for Jenny and himself. Then he wants to add cabins and rent them out as artist studios. Weekly. Monthly."

"And you haven't made this privy to us...why?" Betsy shot from the chair and paced around her living room, avoiding Matilda as she walked around the island. More ideas sprang to mind than a rapid-fire torpedo. If such a thing existed.

"There she goes again, Mary. Betsy's head is getting ready to explode at any minute. Bets, speak to us 'cause if you don't, we'll have a mess to clean up."

"Mary, I can see the tiny cabins as a place for writers too. If Jen and Peter are taking reservations, put me down as their first customer."

"When we finalize the deal, I'll put in a good word for you, Bets. This is why doing a campground is out. As we told you, Jeff and I talked about it, but we can picture this scenario much more than us running an RV Park."

"You'd miss us too much. But you did mention a third Sassy Seconds and it reminded me. Since we're waiting for Ben to get his tires, are we going to find Antonio's sister's place tomorrow?"

"If the men don't have to work, they can come along and take us to lunch."

"Rosie, I don't know about Larry, but Ben's not interested in second-hand stores. The only way you'll get him to go is if you mentioned chocolate. He'd go in a heartbeat."

"Then I guess we'll have to make a stop at the Hershey place on the way there."

CHAPTER TWENTY-FIVE

"Where did you say we're going again?" Ben asked his wife the question right before he pulled his t-shirt over his head the next morning. Then he added, "Have I ever stepped foot in one of these kinds of stores before?"

"We can say you did when you inspected the building that houses Sassy Seconds *Two*. It wasn't an official thrift shop yet, but...oh, and Mary called. She's not feeling well. The four of us will get out of here to let Jeff take care of her. This will be fun."

"Fun is hanging out with Larry and Jeff. Not—"

"Be careful, Mr. Stevenson. Spending the day with Rosie and me might include chocolate. Are sweets incentive enough?"

"It is. And, I'm ready to go." Ben rushed out of the bedroom, down the two stairs and flung the door open to see Larry standing at the bottom of the steps.

"Do we have to do this, Ben?"

"You do, Mr. Wilford." Rose ambled over. "Don't give me any trouble, or I'm bound to do an unchristian-like maneuver. Like hit you over the head with my purse."

"Lar, you better move. She's got things in there that could take you out." Betsy scooted in the backseat of Rose and Larry's vehicle. "I carried it after going through security at the Ft. Myers airport. My left arm is now longer than the right one."

"Betsy, your exaggeration of a situation amazes me. Hush up and buckle your seatbelt. We're on an assignment for the Lord today and time is a wasting. Step on it, Larry."

"Can I get in first?" Ben asked as he got into the backseat of his friend's car. "I have GPS on, Lar. You want it up front?"

"Nah. I can hear it."

Ben wondered if Larry heard the instructions when he passed the street GPS told him to turn at. Thankfully the next instruction said to turn at the next corner.

"You have reached your destination" came out of Ben's phone and Larry pulled into the parking spot next to a shop called Do Over Duds.

"Do Over Duds is by far one of the cutest names I've ever seen for a thrift store. Hurry, Bets, I can't wait to meet Antonio's sister."

The women headed to the shop, but Larry's head swaying from side to side, like a bobble head, held Ben's interest. As they neared the door, his friend quit his moving about and said, "Rosie, you two go on in, we'll visit the adorable shop in a minute, or two. Have to check something on the car."

"Take your time."

ADORABLE SHOP. Larry's changed his meds. Ben kept his eyes on his friend as he strolled back to his car. As if his friend had nothing better to do – Lar kicked the right front tire two or three times.

Ben decided he'd better rush over and check Larry's pulse to see if blood flowed to his I-don't-have-a-mechanical-bone-in-my-body brain. When he got there, he grabbed Larry's wrist, but his friend's laughter halted further movement and he asked, "What's so funny?"

"You. And if you touch me one more time, you'll be the one needing medical attention." He started laughing again.

"When you pull yourself together, please tell me what's going on. You're scaring me. Rose and Bets are probably with me on this. Adorable shop? When have I ever heard you use such terminology?"

"Never, but I'll bet it confused Rosebud. She's in there right now thinking more about my word choices than seeing this lady's shop. Soon enough the ladies will come out and I'll have to tell my wife what I know."

"Again I say, you're scaring me. What do you have to tell Rosie? She doesn't know anything about cars."

"Benjamin, there's nothing wrong with my vehicle, but Sassy Seconds *Two* is in a heap of trouble. A tropical storm is picking Ft. Myers as its target. Shows it'll get the brunt of the storm. The Weather Channel is telling Florida to brace for a doozer."

"And you found humor in this weather forecast?"

"Not really, but your expression then, and now, cracked me up."

"Larry, you're a sick man."

"I've been called worse. But when Rosie finds out about this storm, the only thing able to save the Early Birds and our sanity is the Lord Himself, calming her rattled nerves. I'm praying His touch hits sooner than later."

"I'll add this to our prayer list. How about we head inside?" Ben held the door and his friend took his own sweet time getting there. When Larry passed next to him, he said, "Not an expert, but these things change course. No need to worry about it, but we'll keep praying."

"Keep praying for what?"

"Dear, you're not the only person on the planet who prays. Ben and me, we were exchanging prayer requests and he mentioned Mary needed a little extra since she'd caught a bug." Larry's smile stretched across his face.

"There some kind of something going on, and it's not a flu bug. When Bets and I are done in here, you and your buddy will spill the beans on your sudden interest in 'adorable' thrift shops and praying for others." Rose linked arms with Bets and headed the opposite direction.

"See, Ben. She's done it again. If Rose hears one word out of the ordinary, her radar comes alive and she takes out everyone in her path."

"Sort of like the tropical storm..." Ben chuckled, but stopped and surveyed the scene around him. No chance Rose heard what he'd said. The ladies stood at the counter.

"Benjamin, this isn't at all comical."

"Now I'm the one finding adversity funny. Guess I can understand where you were coming from earlier. Even though, Larry, I still think you're few cups shy of a full gallon." Ben's laughter spilled out again.

"Don't talk. At least I have a spare tire and I saw your jack tucked in the back of my compartment the other day."

Ben inched closer to his friend. "Lar, whatever it is you think you've seen, it's not my jack. I also hate to break it to you, but you don't have a spare either. Jeff said the Class Cs don't come with them. You have to buy them separately."

Larry scanned the ceiling as if he thought he'd find the tire up in the exposed A/C vents. Ben stayed still, not wanting to cause the older man any more pain, but when Larry asked, "What? You're kidding? Right?"

"Wish I was. We're all a bunch of tireless old men traveling on life's highway."

Despite the circumstances of the last half hour, Ben appreciated Larry found humor in his last statement and didn't end up decking him for saying it.

"I'm always afraid to leave you two alone." Betsy came and stood next to Ben. "But it looks like you're having as much fun as we are. However, Larry, you need to stop your wife from buying an item. Another lady and she are fighting over who saw it first."

Larry took off and Ben tagged along to see what Rosie found. They reached the counter at the same time and he heard his friend's wife, "I spied this stylish, yet interesting, bag from across the room. I believe it's mine."

"Rosebud,—"

"Don't mean to interrupt, sir, but I'll ask you a simple question. Who's holding it?" A woman's arms clutched the colorful item.

"You are. But sis, you almost knocked me to the cement floor when you snatched it out of my hands. I have the wounds to prove it. Angel, since you own this place, can you check your surveillance footage? It'll show I won the prized purse."

Angel disappeared behind the curtain, but Ben heard something resembling a noise that Rosie made on more than one occasion. He then assessed the bag in question and lost the ability to control his gaiety.

His quick peek introduced him to pictures of Jesus, which graced the outside of the tote. In one, the King of kings was surrounded by the five thousand. Or little dots for their heads. Next one, the Lord stood outside a door. The picture below it, He held a lone sheep in His arms.

The complete Bible story in one carry on.

Ben had never seen so many depictions of His Savior on something you'd carry your belongings in. And he'd never fathom a woman wanting to cart the bag around for others to see. He figured that in itself was the reason why the item ended up at the second-hand store.

The shop owner returned and took her place behind the register again. From Ben's vantage point, she continued to contemplate her next statement to Rose. Nothing registered in his mind on how to find out who got to take the vibrant purse home.

Larry never gave Angel a chance to respond. He laid a ten on the counter and pronounced, "Rose, I'm buying whatever you call this thing, but I'm giving it to the woman holding it. You have too many bags already and I don't want this one in my RV."

"Can I take a picture of it?"

"By all means." The other lady laid it on the counter and stepped away.

Ben thought Rosie might nab it and run, but instead, she seemed to snap more photos of it than the monuments they'd seen on their visit to Washington, DC. When she put her phone in her pocket she smiled and said, "I hope it's going to a good home."

"It is." The woman picked up the bag again. "Mom and I visited here the other day. When I came out of the dressing room, she was holding it. Since she's sight impaired, the bright colors must have caught her attention. I wanted to buy her the purse, but she said she didn't need it. I came in today to get it."

"And, honey, my husband buying it for you is the best decision he's made in years. Other than marrying me. I'll be praying for you and your mom. Can I give you a hug?"

Rosie's about-face concerning the bag didn't surprise Ben and in the end, she'd made a new friend and got to hug another unsuspecting human being.

"Rosebud?"

"I know. I know. You three go on out to the car. I'll be right with you."

~~~

"Larry, if you haven't noticed, your wife made her mark again." Betsy chuckled as she settled in the backseat of their friend's car.

"You've never said truer words. And she makes me wonder what she's doing in there, while we're sitting out here waiting."

"She's finishing her business with Angel. You know Rose. She's giving her the Sassy Seconds *Two's* information, Linda's in Mississippi and Jenny's in Estes Park. Rosie's on a mission to put their plaques and paintings in as many stores as possible across the U.S.A."

"There might not be a Sassy Seconds *Two* if this

year's hurricane season has anything to say about it. One's brewing as we speak."

"Does Rose know about this?" Betsy paused after she asked the question then proclaimed the obvious, "Of course she doesn't know anything or she'd be doing more than tackling an unsuspecting woman in a thrift store for the lively ensemble piece."

All three laughed, but Bets imagined when Rose found out what churned in the Atlantic, she'd want to do what Floridians do—head to the Sunshine State and board up their homes and businesses.

"You're awful quiet back there. You must be thinking what I'm thinking. Larry hasn't said anything, but there's a possibility we'll need to head south."

Betsy opened up Mr. Pickle's email and read it to him. "We can't go, Ben. After I send the corrections, my book's coming out. Then the book signings." Betsy's mind spun in more directions than the upcoming storm.

Her next thought and less logical, concerning her book, which she kept to herself. *We have to go with them to help. Don't we?*

"The good news, it's not landing tomorrow, or next week. I'll get in touch with Everly and Douglas and ask them to board up the windows and whatever else they need to do to prepare."

"Prepare for what, Larry?" Rose stuck her head in her hubby's window. "I heard you say you're praying and now you're preparing. What is going on?"

Betsy wished the men had been looking straight ahead and not at her. Then they'd have seen Rose coming. But, no, she caught them red-handed, whipping up their own trail of trouble.

After a dramatic show of stomping around the vehicle, Rose plopped down in the passenger's seat. "I'm all ears."

Instead of answering, Larry stretched his arms into the back seat, and made a noise similar to someone yawning. Betsy had seen him do strange movements to prolong the inevitable before, but this one surpassed them all.

Then Bets thought he might want her to slip him a note to help him out of the hurricane-force-winds about to explode next to him. But her brain remained blank as to what to say in the time she had to compose a solution.

Then it hit her and she said, "Larry, work with me." Betsy moved his right arm and placed it on Rose's shoulder. "A little more to the right and you have it. Now give your sweetie a hug and tell her what's going on in Florida."

"Thanks, Bets."

"You're welcome."

"Rosie, we're watching a little disturbance in the Atlantic. It's a tropical s—"

"Mr. Wilford, you're a terrible liar. Everly alerted me while I was in the store about what's going on. They've got it handled. Anything else bothering you?"

Larry's arm shot off of his wife's shoulder. "Yes, you are. Do you know how much energy I wasted trying to figure out how to tell you about this thing?"

"More than you needed to, but in the future I'd suggest you work towards more forthrightness. Just tell me next time."

"I can say the same for you, Rosie."

"You can, but why I didn't tell you I knew you'd be

so much fun to watch while you're figuring out the words to tell me. Example: Little storm. I don't know, but I think one lacked a bit of dramatics." Rose snorted.

"Dramatics? You won the award for it today, dear." Larry chuckled as he pulled his car out of the parking lot. "I can't believe you'd ask the store owner to check her videotapes to find out if you owned the u-g-l-y piece of whatever it was. Seriously?"

"If you promise not to laugh, and I mean all of you. I'll tell you why I seemed out of sorts about the bag. Promise me?" Rose peered over her glasses.

Betsy chimed in, "Whatever you say, I won't so much as snicker." Ben and Larry said, "Ditto" at the same time.

"Okay then. Here goes." Rose stared ahead while she spoke. "I'm in full thrift store mode, whatever it looks like. Betsy and I, we had split up to see more of the store in less time.

My phone beeped and it's from Everly.

"I'm thinking she's checking in, but what do my eyes behold but the words, "I'm sure you've seen this, but if you haven't, click on the attachment from the Weather Channel for the update."

"You clicked on it, didn't you?"

"I did, and it scared me so bad. Larry, that's when everything turned a grayish hue around me. All except the Jesus bag. It's bright colors and the pictures shouted at me to latch onto it. At all costs. I'm afraid something snapped when the woman came up and took it off the hook."

At least a minute elapsed and no one said anything about Rosie's revelation. Bets wanted to reach and pull her friend's hair, but stopped when a loud sniff came from the front seat. Next, she caught Rose getting a tissue out of her purse.

Rosie dabbed at her eyes. "I'm waiting. Doesn't anyone have anything smart-alecky to add? A retort for when my boldness almost sent me to the slammer? If none of you say anything, I'll know you've gone off the deep end."

"Not touching it. No way." Larry made a right into the campground. "Ben, how about you? You want to add anything?"

Words idled on the tip of Betsy's tongue, ready to hit the airwaves. But when the Wilford's car pulled into the RV Park, and she saw Jeff running toward them, she didn't see a need to comment on Rose's blip on the radar.

Larry pulled in and once he stopped, their friend flung the car door open. "Lar, have you seen the forecast on the Weather Channel?"

"To answer your question, Jeff, we've heard about the storm. Thanks to Everly and Douglas, but from the way your face looks, Florida is no longer attached to the lower part of the United States."

CHAPTER TWENTY-SIX

"How about we gather at our place and catch the latest on the storm. Then we'll know what's—" Ben felt his phone vibrate and he checked the text. "The rest of you go on in. Roadside service is on their way. While you're watching TV, I'll be installing my spare tire."

"With our help."

"Larry, do you think it's safe to let the women watch the coverage alone?" Jeff laughed then added, "Not saying they'd embellish the findings, but…"

"Rose already made the evening news with her hurricane hysterics at the second-hand store. We'll tell you all about it when my hubby and the two of you get done out here. As with most things Rosie does, this is one of her best." Betsy nudged her friend. "It's the truth."

"Jeff, I'm telling you, Jesus showed up today. Don't listen to their ridiculous rendering of what happened. Yes, I may have frolicked about in a public place, but a possible hurricane tends to alter one's psyche." Rose climbed the steps into the 5th wheel, with Bets right behind her.

Ben thought they'd make it inside, but no, Rose had one more thing on her mind. "Jeff, I forgot to ask, "how's Mary doing? Hope she's better. Tell her to come over and we'll fix her chicken noodle soup. It always hits the spot when you're not feeling well."

"Thought your specialty was turtle soup, Rosie?" Jeff countered.

Mary came out of their RV. "Noodle soup sounds wonderful. I'll be right over, but first I have to grab my box of tissues."

"Lar, why don't you and Jeff go on in. I've got this handled."

"Are you sure? We might find your stash of chocolates."

"I'll guarantee Betsy and Rose have dived in and are swimming in the candy bars as we stand here talking, Larry. You better hurry."

Ben laughed as his friends headed to his RV. He then walked over to his vehicle to meet the tow truck. The young man sprang out of the cab. "Hi, I'm Todd. Says here on the work order that I'm fixing one of the back inside tires and installing a spare. Am I correct?"

"Son, if you want to crawl around on the ground, you go for it." Ben's back appreciated the man taking over the job.

Todd removed both tires and put the one in need of repair on the tailgate of his truck. He made several trips to the side to retrieve the tools he needed. As he tried to put a tool between the tire and rim, Ben noticed the young man's hands shook.

He must have seen him staring and commented, "Had a stroke last year. I'm doing better and I'm thankful my boss allows me to work in the field. Mr.

Graves calls it my physical therapy." Todd chuckled.

Ben wanted to ask him more questions, but Todd interrupted his thoughts. "Mr. Stevenson, I see the problem. Your valve stem is loose and it's too short. I'll put you in a longer one and it'll be easier to get to when you need air again. I'll check the others too."

"Todd, I read almost every day on Facebook about blowouts. Better keep a closer watch on my tires from now on. Not smart that I didn't catch this."

"Another reason to have roadside assistance." Todd fixed the valve stem then lifted the tire off and rolled it to the side of Ben's truck. In less than fifteen minutes, he finished the job and wiped his hands on a towel he'd taken from the side pocket of his work truck.

While he put his tools away, Ben rummaged in his wallet and gave Todd the two twenties he'd hid for times like these. "Son, thanks for changing out the other ones. You saved me from making another service call. Next time might have been more eventful than this one."

"All in a day's work. Appreciate the tip. It'll help pay for a book I need for my final class this summ—". Todd stopped and raced to the cab of his truck. A minute later he yelled, "Sorry, got to run. Another call. Be careful out there."

Ben waved as Todd's truck disappeared and the issues of the day hit him. "I'd like to ask why things happen the way they do, Lord, but I'll trust You know what You're doing. Please calm what's going on in the Atlantic. While You're at it, heal Todd. He's a good man. Amen."

"You coming in to eat sometime today? Soup's ready."

Betsy's smile at their opened door hurried his steps and the sweet smell of brownies cooking in the convection oven greeted him too. Ben's stomach growled as he entered and he said, "Can I have dessert first?"

"You need to hush. We're listening to the Weather Channel. An update just came in." Rose moved closer to the TV.

Ben put his attention on the soup in front of him as he crumpled crackers into his bowl. While the others peered at the screen, Ben devoured his meal and kept a watchful eye on the goodies cooking two feet in front of him.

"The tropical storm is strengthening, but it's still too early to tell if it'll make a turn and go back out in the Atlantic. Stay tuned for the next update."

Ding.

Ben heard the oven timer go off, but as he reached for the handle, Rose's arm appeared. "The brownies have to cool or the edges won't harden, which we all know is the best part. Step away from the oven."

She opened the door and took the pan out and set it on the back burner. Rose then acted as if she guarded the crowned jewels of a small foreign country and not the dessert they'd enjoy later.

"Don't know how you got over here so fast on those short little legs of yours." Ben smiled at their height-deprived friend, "but as you know—I prefer my brownies gooey." He held up his spoon. "Yep. Right out of the oven."

"Touch those brownies, Benjamin, and I'll have Betsy searching for more than your box of bandages."

Ben did the bait and switch with Rosie at the

stovetop and accomplished what he'd set out to do—to snatch a bite out of the center of the brownie.

"Never thought I'd hear myself say this, but you're more of a brat than your wife."

"That's the nicest thing you've ever said to me, Rose."

"Hey, once again I'm hearing every word you're saying about me."

"Bets, your husband has no mercy on me or Larry, and the peril we're in. If he did, he'd back away from the one thing able to soothe my fears. Which I'm going to devour in one swift swoop and not even wipe my mouth if I'm messy."

"Rosebud. I'm not a meteorologist, but my prediction – this will fizzle out and we'll continue our trip up the east coast. There's more sights out there to see."

"Says you. I'm not taking any chances, mister. I'm leaving here in the morning. With or without you." Rose picked up the knife next to the stove and cut a section out of the brownie then stuffed half of it in her mouth.

As soon as she did, her eyes widened. Ben grabbed a glass next to the sink and filled it with water. "Here. Drink this before you choke to death."

"And when she's done washing down everyone else's dessert, we're going home to discuss our future travel plans. The ones where all of the Early Birds are heading north. North to Maine."

Larry's red face, as he sat on the loveseat, almost caused Ben to jog to his friend's RV to get his blood pressure medicine ready. But he decided to stay to hear Rosie's reply, which never came. Instead, she put the brownie she'd taken on a paper plate and strolled to the door. "You coming, dear?"

Ben observed movement from Larry he hadn't seen in years. Or a spring sprung in Betsy and his loveseat. Whatever the case, their friend got off of it and sprinted to the door and down the stairs in record time.

On the last step, he glanced back and said, "One of you might want to check on us in about ten minutes. I'll either need those bandages Rosie talked about, or my wife will be in a coma from consuming too much chocolate."

~~~

"Will do, Lar. And Rosie – you behave yourself." Betsy closed the door and leaned against it. "Can you believe those two?"

"And if I know Rosie, she is giving him the business. The gusts emitting from her are measuring close to those of the storm stirring in the ocean. At this exact moment."

Betsy laughed at her hubby's comment and added, "do you think we ought to go over and check on them? She sounded serious this time. The Early Birds might be down one member, as we're sitting here chatting."

Jeff piped up, "Lar can hold his own. I'd suggest we let them alone to figure it out and I'll bet we'll be on the road, as our friend Larry said earlier, "We'll be heading north to Maine.""

"Or not." Betsy spied the words on her phone. "Rose says they're southbound tooo-morrrrrr-ooooow morning."

"Okay, we need to intervene." Jeff's long legs carried him the short distance to the door. "Is anyone else coming?"

"I'm right behind you." Betsy wanted to whack her friend up side her head for heading into a possible hurricane. But the real reason for perpetrating harm—her BFF had forgotten about her big news.

Seemed *Always Enjoy the Journey* slipped everyone's mind.

CHAPTER TWENTY-SEVEN

"Rose, have you lost what's left of your mind?" Betsy shouted the words after she flung open the Wilford's door. "People evacuate when they hear a hurricane is coming their way. Not the other way around. Can we talk some sense into you? Now about my bo—"

"About my wife making sense, Bets, good luck with that. Why don't all of you come in and we'll see what we can do to change Rose's mind."

"Y'all can talk until the Lord steps on earth again, but I'm heading south. Do any of you want to know why I'd head into the storm and not away from it?"

"We'd love to know, but don't say a word until we're inside to hear it." Betsy took her seat at the banquette, next to Ben. Jeff and Mary pulled in on the other side of it. Larry rested his behind on the edge of the bed. And Rose planted herself in front of their tiny stove.

"Okay, Rosie, you're on."

"I don't have to take a vote to know you all think I'm nuts for what I'm about to propose. You're welcome to come, but I'll understand if you don't. I do have to digress and say I never thought I'd be the one to leave the Early Birds first."

"As far as I'm concerned, we're not leaving the group. Secondly, you still haven't told us why you want to head into harm's way?" Larry gestured towards the banquette. "We'd all love to hear your plan."

"Keep your shorts on and hush. I'm getting to it." Rose walked to the couch and patted the seat next to her. "How about you come over and I'll tell you all about it."

"I can't wait." Larry took a seat next to her and said, "Proceed."

"In a nutshell—if the storm continues to intensify or it dribbles to a tiny rainstorm, I want to be there to give our assistance, wherever it may be needed."

"We're in, said the Stevenson's."

"Us too."

Rose broke out into a wide grin. "That was easy. However, Bets didn't vote."

"I'm waiting to find out who Ben is riding down to Florida with – you or does Jeff and Mary want him to tag along with them?"

"Where will you be?"

"At my book signing Mr. Pickle is setting up for me. Remember? I do hope the campground I find have pull-through sites 'cause I don't want to try and back the 5er into one of them by myself."

Betsy hoped no one else sensed her sassiness in her words. However, from the extent of her husband and friend's stares, they each tried to figure out a way to calm the next typhoon brewing in an RV Park in Hershey, Pennsylvania. This one named Hurricane

Betsy.

~~~

Anything Ben said implicated him in the crime of forgetfulness. Flat out. He'd forgotten his wife's colossal news of getting her debut novel published. And the book signings to follow. *Oh, Lord, I'm in deep trouble.*

"Betsy, can you ever forgive me?" Rosie's bottom lip jutted out. "I've only been thinking about what I want. Not asking anyone else what they want to do. And now I've failed my bestest friend on her largest accomplishment?"

"Put Jeff and me down on the thoughtless list too."

Ben scooted closer to Betsy, even though they already sat elbow to elbow. He reached for her hand. "Add my name too. If you're giving out ribbons for insensitive people today, I'd win the top prize."

"You and everyone else sitting in here, Benja—"

"I appreciate everyone's admittance of wrong doing, but Larry, please let my hubby grovel a bit more. He's doing such a fine job." Betsy smiled then added, "And just so you know, this will make for a stupendous scene in my next book."

"Who knew we'd be famous for our absentmindedness. You can also add into your story that we'll be continuing our travels with you. Betsy, there's no way you can sign anything without me sitting beside you." Rose snorted as she walked back over to the stove.

Betsy's scrunched forehead told Ben his wife worked on a response to her friend's comment, but nothing came out. He wanted to come to her aid. Say something witty, but in the end Larry got up from the couch and stood next to Rose and said, "Are you sure?"

"Yes I am, despite what I spouted off earlier. Another thing, the Lord wouldn't want me to desert my BFF. Friendship outweighs an itsy bitsy storm in the tropics. We'll weather whatever comes our way."

"Which concludes our meeting and I'm taking my wife home." Jeff picked up the tissue box in front of Mary and they made their way to the door. "Let us know if plans change. My GPS goes north or south."

"Take it from me, the Early Birds are packing up and heading northeast when we hear from Mr. Pickle." Ben helped Betsy up from the banquette and gave her a hug. "Isn't that right, dear?"

"Absolutely."

"And while we're at it," Rose held her hand in the air. "we'll praise the Lord for taking care of the pesky storm we're worrying so much about."

~~~

While Betsy changed into her pj's, Rosie's comments about helping others stirred inside her head and she made her own decision. "I'll make the corrections Mr. Pickle sent me. Book signings can happen anywhere. No big deal. Heading south is more important."

Now time to brush her teeth, but she found she'd squeezed out a hefty amount on her toothbrush. Betsy attempted to stuff the paste back into the container. Impossible.

"Hon, did you fall asleep in there?"

Ben's question made her fling the toothbrush across the tiny room. She watched it slide down the glass door of their shower, leaving a trail of aqua blue toothpaste all the way to the floor.

"Betsy, I hear you in there. Are you coming to bed? Tonight?"

"Be right with you. Had a tiny catastrophe." *Which you caused.* Betsy left the last part unsaid and finished cleaning up. As she made her way to the bedroom, the pocket of her pj pants beeped.

"I'll bet Rosie changed her mind."

Oh how Betsy wanted to chuckle at Ben's comment, but read Rose's message out loud instead. 'We're *on the road again.* Sign! Sign! Sign loads of books, little lady. Praise the Lord Almighty.'"

Boy is she, and everyone else, going to be surprised when I drop my bombshell. Betsy settled on her side of the bed and took a couple of breaths. "Mr. Stevenson, do you think it's too late to call another Early Birds meeting?"

~~~

Either Ben's hearing needed checked or his wife asked him to call a meeting at 11:00 at night. The determined look she wore sent him into action. No questions asked.

"That's what I said. My beloved wants you two to come over. Right now." Ben listened as Larry told him he'd be over in what he had on and Ben urged him, "please put your robe on first. The RV Park has rules about such things."

Ben laughed as he hung up then called Jeff. "Betsy's calling an emergency Early Birds meeting. ASAP. Appropriate clothing required."

Jeff assured him he'd put on something presentable, but added. "Mary's sleeping, so I don't think I'll wake her."

In less than five minutes the others in the group

gathered in Ben and Betsy's living room. He had to say none appeared too chipper, but his cohorts sat clothed and appeared ready to hear his wife's dissertation. He waited with baited breath himself.

"I've called you here at this late hour to propose a change. I've checked the Weather Channel and if it doesn't wobble, Fl-or-i-da will have damage. How severe, is still a question, but I vote we head south. Anything with my books can happen anywhere."

"No. No. And in Jesus' Holy Name. No."

"Rose, I've made up my mind. Mr. Pickle will have to schedule my book events for the southern states. Next year we'll finish going up the east coast as we proposed to do this year."

Ben listened to his wife's words and her doggedness reminded him of when she'd told him, "I'm going to write for a living." However, this time she seemed a little too anxious to head in a different direction.

Which meant one thing—Betsy had started to listen to the wrong voices in her head again. Ben heard the words, "Impending storms override progress of my book. Thank goodness." He had to reel her in.

And he did, when his wife quit selling them on her grand idea. "Hon, you don't have to convince us, and if we talk much longer, daylight will have arrived and we can take off, which we won't. My question to all of us is: What does the Lord want us to do?"

"He wants us to help our fellow man."

"Correct, but with all the waffling going on, it seems we've forgotten to ask Him where He wants us. I'm pretty sure Betsy and my situation is set on us heading north. The rest of you have to figure out which direction you're going. Where's the Lord leading you?"

"Ben, I'm glad someone with some sense has spoken." Rose rolled the office chair she occupied over to Betsy. "And your hubby's right, you have your course set. And the rest of us – we need to put the Lord back where He belongs. First and foremost."

Rose then took off on a prayer alerting the heavenly realm that what she brought to their attention took precedence over wars, famine, or the national debt. No one, including Ben, emitted a sound during her petition on their behalf.

"Amen and amen."

"Rose, I don't know if Ben's roof withstood your petitioning, but if I was a tropical storm – I'd stay clear of you." Jeff clamored to his feet. "I better get back to my wife. Check if her cold is road worthy. Whichever way we go."

"Betsy, you and I, are staying in Pennsylvania where you'll sit down and revise your work. Then you'll send it back to Mr. Pickle."

"Keep us posted, Ben."

The Early Birds made a quick exit and Ben turned to his wife. Her face resembled a ripe tomato, which meant one thing. He'd plunged himself into boiling water with his statement of staying put. *And my infraction of forgetting my wife's soon-to-be-published novel.*

CHAPTER TWENTY-EIGHT

The late hour had no bearing on Betsy's decision to walk out of the living room and leave her hubby sitting on their loveseat. She disappeared behind their bedroom door and tried to swallow the disagreeable words, wanting to spill forth for whoever wanted to listen.

That was until she heard a knock on the door. Betsy ignored it until she heard, "Mom, I know you're in there. You might not know this but Dad's sorry for his present and past sins inflicted upon you. Whenever they might have happened."

Betsy heard her husband's high-pitched voice, but the noise at her feet made her look down. There she saw their pooch's paw moving from side to side, almost as if she waved at her, under the large gap in their bedroom door. Bets lost all control, but managed to open the door.

"Hi, Mom, is Dad forgiven, or does he have to get on his hands and knees again and walk across the kitchen floor?"

"Quit it or I'll send both of you over to the Wil—" Betsy's laughter drowned out the rest of Larry and

Rosie's last name. When she composed herself, she said, "As hard as it is for me to say this, yes, I forgive you, Benjamin. Anyone who talks through a dog can't be all bad."

This statement sent Betsy into more chuckles. Each time she thought she'd gotten a handle on her laughter, the image of their precious pooch's paw or Ben's animated voice came to mind.

Betsy had to share the latest with her friend. She peered out of the window to check the back of Rosie's RV. The bedroom light shone bright. "Ben, I'll be in the living room. I need to do something."

She called Rose this time and for the next ten minutes, they tossed funnies across the airwaves. Until her friend broached the inevitable topic of the Early Birds spreading their wings and the possibility of them going in two different directions.

"Hello, Betsy. Did you fall asleep or did aliens snatch you up from your RV?"

"Rosie, I'm right here on the loveseat, waiting for the Lord to expedite His answer on what we should do." Betsy whispered the words, hoping Ben didn't hear their conversation clear up in their bedroom.

"The Lord's going to tell you what I said." Ben came down the stairs.

"Bets, I recall you telling me years ago, 'I'm writing for the Lord. If my words touch one person, fine with me.' Your book is your ministry and it IS important. It's as essential as going south to help—'"

"Ben, I don't want to bring up your previous sins I said I forgave five minutes ago, but how crucial is my book to the human race? To refresh your memory, you and the other five Early Birds, are my closest friends, and everyone forgot it even existed?"

"How about we resume this fun conversation in the morning. Tell Rosie you'll talk to her tomorrow and come to bed."

Betsy said her goodbyes then shut off her phone. *Yes, it's going to be a long night. Lord, I hope You're awake.*

~~~

Abbreviated prayers worked, or Ben hoped they did on his way to their bedroom. Tonight's plea—help in understanding his wife. One minute she wanted to go south with nary a mention about her book. Next, she's angry at them because it slipped their minds.

Ben moved their sleeping pooch over and got back in bed. A glance at the clock told him he'd be sorry in the morning for such a late night. *Sometimes discussions take time, but 2:30 is pushing it in my book.*

The minute Ben uttered the word 'book', Betsy's novel popped into his mind and he thought, *Lord, come be our guest on our late-night extravaganza.*

"You asleep up here?" Betsy's voice and footsteps sounded outside their bedroom door.

"Waiting for you."

"And praying many impassioned prayers to make sense out of this evening, I'm sure."

Ben laughed. "You know me too well."

"I know it's late, but can we talk?"

"Ah huh." Ben's real choice swayed toward lying flat, with his head on his pillow asleep, but Betsy's swollen eyes suggested they'd stay up and talk. He waited, but must have nodded off. When Betsy spoke, it seemed far off. Ben shook his head then said, "Is it time to get up?"

"No, and since you were sleeping while I shared my heart, I'll have to repeat myself."

Ben laughed as he scooted to his wife's side of the bed. "I'm awake. Go ahead, sweetums."

"Ben, you gave me a look at the Wilford's and it said a number of things. First: I'm trying to sabotage my writing. Second: I don't want to go to the book signings. The reason being: in case no one shows up. Third: It said I'm not spending enough time with the Lord."

"One of my looks said all that. I am good."

"You are and it's time to go to sleep. Good night, dear. Oh, I forgot, it's your turn to pray tonight. Or this morning. Whatever day you choose."

"Amen."

"Amen goes at the end of most prayers."

"It does, doesn't it?" He prayed, leaving nothing in their part of the world untouched. After a minute or two, he sent hallelujahs up to heaven since the love of his life's breathing had steadied. She'd fallen asleep. "Sweet dreams, my love."

~~~

"Pancakes for everyone." Rose's words emitted from Betsy's phone when she answered it.

"Tell me again, Ben, why don't I leave it plugged in downstairs? I don't 'cause I'd miss a vitally important call, inviting me to breakfast five hours after I hit the sack."

"Your grumbling isn't helping my sleep either. Did I hear someone say, "pancakes?""

"You did and have at them. I'm staying here and maybe I'll dream of me eating them and they'll fill me up."

"Come on. Get your tail moving. We only have a day or two with them, if we're lucky." Ben saw Betsy's sour expression then added. "And before her coffee, my wife does not care if her best friends leave in five minutes."

"Yes, I do, but where is my coffee?"

"In the pot downstairs. Oh, let me go get you some."

Betsy lay in bed, anticipating her favorite beverage. And her friends leaving. If given the chance to write the scene—she'd fail miserably at capturing the amount of drama on their final day together.

Bets willed herself to put both feet on the carpet. "No need to think about that right now. I'm in dire need of coffee. And pancakes, which Rose informed me at too early of an hour. Oh, I also need clothes." She picked a random shirt out of her closet.

"Coffee, my dear."

"Huh?"

Betsy laughed as her hubby shifted his phone to his left hand. "I wasn't talking to you, Larry. I was handing Betsy her mug and you'll be glad to know it's high octane. It'll get her going. As far as I can tell, we'll arrive at your place in about ten minutes."

"Larry, tell Ben to tell Bets we have plenty of sugar since she's not a fan of syrup. Unless she's sitting down to write a romance novel. The syrupy the subject matter the better. Gotta run." Rose closed with her signature noise.

The urge to yell, "Southward Ho" almost overtook Betsy while she tied her tennis shoes, but uttered instead, "Lord, You're in control of all situations, but what will we do without our friends?"

"You'll trust in Him and sign, sign, sign books. I stole Rose's line and while we're at it, I'll tag along as your new best friend and momentous marketing guru." Ben joined her on the edge of the bed.

Ben's words comforted her, but what made Betsy smile was when Matilda jumped on the bed and climbed up and licked her ear. Then their adorable Boston Terrier mix pushed her way in between them and rested her chin on Betsy's knee.

"How does she know the exact time we need her to calm the mayhem surrounding us?"

"Our precious pooch has a perceptive personality."

"She does and I need to proceed to my laptop pronto. Mr. Pickle may have provided...I have no idea of a 'p' word to replace 'email'. Well poop."

"Check them quick 'cause I like my pancakes hot off the griddle. The glob of butter melting off the sides. Syrup warmed to—"

"Perfection and if you head out our door and start walking—I'll be right behind you." Betsy opened her emails on her phone and realized she hadn't looked at them the day before. The only response after seeing Mr. Pickle's email, "Oops. I'm in trouble now."

"And a less-hungry husband asks, 'What can I help you with, my sweetness?'" Ben spun around at the door.

"Nothing, dear. Go enjoy your pancakes. I'll grab one of the granola bars to tide me over while I read."

Betsy heard the door close and loved Ben for not saying anything pertaining to her procrastination. The marked-up manuscript loomed at her fingertips and her assignment for the day—rework it and send it to Mr. Pickle. *Then I'll have a published book to hold in my hands.*

Her phone beeped and Bets smiled. "Lord, You have impeccable timing. And keep me on the straight and narrow road." Betsy checked the text Ben wrote, "U R only correcting mistakes. Not rewriting."

Betsy sent a happy face to her hubby then replied to Mr. Pickle, with a short note apologizing. She promised he'd receive the new-and-improved manuscript tomorrow and added to herself. "I hope it soothes out the wrinkles of my forgetting."

Bets opened the manuscript with all of its markings. Her breathing quickened and before she made a correction, she prayed for clarity and nerves of steel to change what the editors suggested.

Peace and determination flowed through her and Betsy began the task. Each page had multiple changes, but easy fixes. One scene flew over the head of the editors and Bets spent almost an hour reworking it.

Just a few more tweaks…

Betsy reread the new words she put down and shouted, "Praise You, Jesus. We're on a roll." This caused her to chuckle and she realized her one character would say the same thing at any given time or circumstance.

Her phone beeped again and she wanted to ignore it, but picked it up. Rosie's face filled the screen. After swiping to answer, Betsy said, "Hello, you do know you're obstructing forward progress, don't you?"

"I'm calling to tell you we're holding a prayer vigil about you. Goodbye."

Betsy saw her friend reach to turn her phone off and before she accomplished it said, "I'd guessed since I hadn't seen my hubby, you were up to something. Hey,

I have an idea. To give me more time, why don't you go help humanity. You can tell me all about it when you return."

"Are you positive you want to miss our last H.H.H. until the Early Birds meet again? It won't be the same without you."

"I'm sure it won't." Betsy laughed. "But this way, tomorrow and the next day, we can do all the bonding we can muster before you hit the road without us. Then we'll stay here and I'll become widely successful at my funner-than-fun book signings. The ones you will miss."

"We have our own problems. Hurricanes. Floods. But oh, how she goes on and on and on. Bets, since you also do it with your writing, I'd suggest you set a timer. It'll remind you to get up and not have rigor mortis set in your joints."

With no need to expound on her diagnosis, she ignored her friend's comment and said, "Have Ben bring over Matilda and she'll have me hopping every three or four hours to take her out."

"Goodbye, dear, and know whatever we do today, we will miss you."

Betsy stuck her phone in the file cabinet. Away from any more interruptions from friends or hubby. Then it dawned on her, in a couple of days, that would be their only way of communicating. "I'm not going to cry. I'll save the tears for when I see their taillights leaving the camp ground."

CHAPTER TWENTY-NINE

In all of Ben's days, and from the frightening stares from the other Early Birds, they'd never been a part of a H.H.H. like that day. He didn't wait for the others. His wife needed to hear all the details of what happened to them.

"Betsy, you're never going to—"

"Benjamin Stevenson, you better put a sock in it until we all get in there. Don't you dare tell her anything." Rose came into their 5th wheel and her smile lit up the whole room.

"Jeff, Mary and I are bringing up the rear. Today's escapade made what little hair I have to curl up and spring forth."

"Larry, I beg your pardon, but there's not enough hair up on your head to do anything of the sort. I believe I saw a few strands stuck straight out in the middle of whatever you want to call what we did today."

Mary's comment about Larry's hair sent everyone into a fit of laughter. If metered, it made the Top Ten List for Mirth. On another list, Betsy's scowl ranked #1 and she said, "Since I wasn't part of the messing about today, can someone fill me in?"

"Early Birds, grab a seat. The theatre is again selling tickets to the Early Birds show." Ben put off starting the story until the group got comfortable, knowing each had a part in the malarkey. They'd have plenty to add. "Are we ready?"

"If you don't start soon, I'm going back to my manuscript."

"Betsy, you better get your notepad and pencil ready. This is one you'll want in your next book. Count on it." Rose pointed at Ben. "You're on, Mr. B."

"Hon, we left shortly after Rose called you and we were tooling down the road."

"I spotted a truck broken down up the road."

"Thank you, Larry. I was getting there. Anyway, I didn't ask, but pulled in behind them."

"Ben told us to stay put. He wanted to have all the fun."

"No, Rose, I didn't think we all needed to get out and scare the people to death. I know you – you'd have them in a hug in—"

"Yep and I'll take over the story. Ben goes to the passenger's side door then motioned to us. I heard your hubby say, 'Call 9-1-1.' Bets, my fat little legs ran as fast as humanly possible and what do I see? A young lady and she's about to have her baby on the side of the road."

"While we're waiting for the ambulance, her husband said he'd left his phone at home and hadn't planned on running out of gas." Ben smiled. "I reached for mine to call for help and I'd left mine on the dash. Glad one of us had their phone."

"Betsy, this is where the fun begins. The ambulance didn't come in what I thought was a timely manner. I'm thinking out loud and the word 'Uber' leaves my lips. When I look up from my phone, more eyes are on me than the Kansas City Royals on Opening Day."

"An exaggeration from my wife and I'll continue. I made sure Rosie didn't click on the Uber app, but things started to get more serious and out of all of our league. Then Lucy's water broke and I'm no expert, but—"

"That moved things along a bit, Larry." Ben laughed when he remembered his friend's wide-eyed expression and him backing away from the truck.

"It does hurry things and Uber was back on the table in my mind when the EMTs showed up. They took over. In less than three minutes they had her on a stretcher and inside the ambulance and on their way to the hospital."

"Stop. I have to ask. Uber. Seriously? Rose, they take people to airports, not hospitals."

"Missy, they take you wherever you want to go and this little lady needed transportation – in the worst way." Rose finished with her normal noise.

"Clint rode with us and we followed the flashing lights. People probably thought we were ambulance chasers, but I didn't want to lose them. I got us there, and they rushed Lucy inside. I dropped Clint off at the Emergency room door and a nurse whisked him away too."

"Jeff and Mary, I haven't heard much from you two."

"I kept my distance. Didn't want to give either one of them my cold." Mary sneezed. "See."

"I'm staying back too, but I will tell you—those EMTs knew what they were doing. Thought for a minute I'd be able to write helping to birth a baby on my list of things I never thought I'd do."

"With those big hands of yours, you'd catch it on the way out."

"Lar, today's the closest I ever want to get an opportunity like that again."

"So you obviously stayed at the hospital. What did Lucy have?" Betsy held her pen on the paper.

"A girl named Abigail Rose. Betsy, notice the beautiful middle name. She made her debut forty-five minutes after we arrived and she's A.D.O.R.A.B.L.E."

"And Rosie's head grew six inches around when she heard what they'd named the little one. And she and Mary hurried down to the gift shop and bought out the store of every baby item available to them."

"We did not, Larry. There were boy items Abigail didn't need. Anyway, Mr. Wilford, what do you know about having a baby? Or what they need?"

"About as much as you do, Rose. But this brings up a matter I believe the Early Birds need to discuss. Since another unexpected development has blown our way." Larry laughed then said, "Hope y'all liked my storm-related reference."

"We did and want to hear more."

"Glad you asked, Jeff. I propose we hunker down here tomorrow and get with Clint and Lucy to see if they have all they need to bring Abigail home."

"Mr. Wilford, that's the sweetest thing I've ever heard you say. But since we're inquiring about things – where are we on the main storm brewing in Florida and the reason we were leaving in the first place?"

"The Weather Channel is saying it's still a tropical storm. I talked to Douglas, while we waited at the hospital. He's handling it down there and has secured all the windows and doors. Now we wait like we did during Hurricane Ike in Houston."

"Which left us with lots of tree damage seventy-seven miles inland. Let's see if I have this right. We stay here to insure a new baby has all it needs. Or get ourselves on the road to make sure we still have a business to go to when it blows over."

Rose crossed her arms and tapped her foot. Ben watched the gale force winds start where his friend stood and only God had the ability to put a lid on that pressure cooker. He also noticed Larry stared at his wife. His lips moved, but nothing came out.

"Lar, say whatever you have to say, so we can get this train moving."

"Your lack of...Rosebud, I don't have a word for it, but whatever it is astounds me. You'd leave a poor little defenseless bambino without a onesie to call her own to go see if a building you own—"

"Betsy, you or I don't hold a candle to Lar's performance. A 'onesie to call her own'? Good one, Lar. Didn't know you knew what their little outfits are called. And, yes, when you say it for all to hear – it makes me sound self-centered and I'm so sorry."

"I accept your apology and suggest we regroup tomorrow. Betsy can finish her work and all of us can go to the hospital when visiting hours start in the morning?"

"Works for me, Ben. You know I always love happy endings."

~~~

"She's the cutest thing I've ever seen." Betsy held Abigail the following morning. "And if I wasn't hitting the Big 60 soon, I'd tell Ben I wanted one of these."

"And she'd make me and Mary, Jeff's wife, take care of him or her. Or call us to help her find where she'd left her abandoned baby." Rose put her hand to her mouth and Betsy imagined it helped to keep her hullabaloo under wraps.

"Quit making Lucy laugh." Larry positioned himself between Rose and Betsy. "It also startles our bundle of joy."

"Lar, you do know you had nothing to do with any of this, don't you?"

"I do, but I'm feeling a bit grandfatherly. Let me have a minute."

Betsy's heart almost melted at the older man's declaration. Even Ben seemed to wear an extra big smile. Go figure since he'd always had an aversion to tiny tots. Afraid they'd do one of those baby things on him.

Clint walked in and his grin mirrored Ben's. Betsy walked over to him. "Sir, I believe this preciousness belongs to you."

"She does." He took her and turned to Lucy. "The nurse said they're finishing up our paperwork and we'll be ready to go home." Clint handed Abigail to his wife. "We can't go home. Our truck is—"

"Is gassed up and the car seat is buckled into the back seat, per the directions we found in the box. Relax. You gave us the keys yesterday."

"Oh, yeah." Clint laughed. "Guess my mind was on other things."

"Which brings us to why we're here." Ben stepped

to the side of the bed. "Lucy, what else can the Early Birds do for you? Clint, do you want us to follow you home and fix anything? You'll be too busy figuring out fatherhood to work on projects and Abigail's too young to help."

"No, we'll take it from here. Hello, I'm Pastor Gordon. Clint called us last night and gave us the news. Thank you for stopping to help them."

Betsy spied five people standing at the door and the scene reminded her of when Rose and Larry heard the news on Sassy Seconds *Two*. All of God's children milled about praising Him for what miraculous things He did in their lives. And continued to do.

"Guess we're on our way then." Larry moved towards the door and shook the new visitors' hands. "If there's anything, Clint has my number. Call us, we'll be here until Friday morning."

Betsy hit the down arrow on the elevator and they piled in when it arrived. "Now that's the definition of church. We *are* the hands and feet of Jesus. Come rain, sleet, or hail. The body of Christ is always there to deliver."

"You've stolen the Post Office's slogan, but it works. And speaking of rain, the tropical storm is—"

"Stepping on my last nerve, Larry. From what we watched this morning, it's telling us to get *on the road again*." Rose stopped and her expression aimed at Betsy shouted she had more to say.

Bets waited and when her friend composed herself, she said. "We'll be *on the road again*. Away from our, our frie..." Rose expelled a noise. This time it didn't resemble a snort, but a full-blown Cry-A-Thon.

And Betsy hitched a ride on the parade with her

bestie. By the time the elevator door reopened, they'd reached a crescendo of cosmic proportions. Four men, waiting to get on, gaped at them as if they held the seat as spectators to the pandemonium going on.

"Rose. Betsy. Get a grip. Please." Larry shushed them.

Bets wanted to tell the gawkers the reason for their tears, but Ben's slight push on her back ushered him and her out while the next party filed in. The other three followed and the elevator door shut behind the newest occupants.

"I'll bet we're the topic of conversation on those men's trip up."

"Rose, as always, we're the talk of the town." Betsy flung her arm over her friend's shoulder. "How about the rest of the time, we enjoy each other's company? Boo hooing is for the birds. Oh, that's funny. Birds. Guess we have our new name - the Bye, Bye Birds."

~~~

Ben contemplated their new name and its meaning all the way back to the RV Park. Imagine his surprise when Mary scurried over to the dually. She had the back door open before he'd come to a complete stop and he said, "Jeff, whatever your wife has to tell you must be important."

"It is, but first I want to hear about our little gift from God."

"Mary, you do realize I almost ran over you and your first concern is about Abigail?"

"I have a cold, Ben, and I'm up to my eyeballs in cough syrup. Oh, and why I darted out in front of you, I had a dream of all dreams." Mary chuckled. "And nothing about the dream spells sanity either."

"When my wife has a dream, it's worth listening too. Since they tend towards bizarre. After she gets done telling us this one, have her share the one where she's being shot at while in the backseat of a VW Bug."

"How about we grab lunch in our respective RVs and meet at the picnic table around 2:00."

"Nothing doing, buster. The six of us are thick as honey in a honeycomb. We are spending the rest of today to...geth...er. Side by side. The only time we're apart is when one of us has to use the rest—"

"Don't say it. We get the picture. And so you know, Rose, I'm not staying up half the night to walk down memory lane. We'll have plenty of other times to chew the fat with these people. I'll need my sleep so I'm chipper to drive."

"Lar, you do have a way with words. And I agree, I'd rather you get the proper rest so the light poles we pass won't have to cringe every time you go by one. I'll see them leaning since I'm driving behind you."

"You can lead. Jeffy. Anytime."

"Lose the name and I will."

"Mary, I almost forgot to tell you. Since we're chatting about names, we've changed ours again. Our new name is: Where Are the Birds. Or maybe..."

"Thought we agreed on Bye, Bye Birds."

"Like it too."

"You do come up with them, my dear. Hope the last one doesn't stick for very long."

"Me neither, Mary."

Betsy saw Rosie tear up again, but her friend didn't head south before her Class C carried her there. And to keep her on that road with less crying, Bets suggested, "How about we all go to our RV. Ben will fix us something to eat. Then you can tell us your dream."

The Early Birds followed Betsy inside and in no time Ben had a meat and cheese plate, crackers and all the fixings out on the table. "Brunch is served."

Manners flew out the window as they filled their plates at the table. Ben stole crackers off Larry and Jeff's plate and a piece of Swiss cheese off Rosie's. Mary slipped three olives on Betsy's and a yelp came out of her that scared Matilda.

"Don't yell until you give them a try."

"Not happening in this lifetime. Maybe when I get to heaven, Mary."

Betsy sat at her desk and wanted this day to go on forever. To find a way to lock the door and not let these silly people out of her RV. Even for a little while. And if she didn't concentrate on her plate of food soon, and start eating, she'd be going down the tearful turnpike.

"Don't know what she is thinking, but she's not with us anymore." Rose reached over and took the green olives off Betsy's plate. "Hello, is anyone home?"

"I am and I'm ready to hear Mary's dream."

Mary put the cracker she held on her plate and smiled, "I have to do a disclaimer before I tell it to you. The mental state of some of us might take this for action, so promise me we'll steer clear of precipices."

"Stevenson's, for sure.

"The Miller's second it."

"Wilford's, neither of them like heights." Rose laughed. "Go on with your dream."

"The Early Birds are ready to go and have said our goodbyes to Ben and Betsy. I wave out the window at them and the CB goes off. "Breaker 21."

Jeff answers Larry and we hear, "Let's turn around. I have an idea."

"We make a U-turn and Larry jumps out when he stops. The next thing I see is the Stevenson's hooking up their 5er and getting in their truck. Lar gets in and motions us to follow him."

"Where on earth is my hubby taking us?"

"Hold on, Rosie. It gets better." Mary took a bite of a cracker then added after she swallowed. "I needed nourishment to finish my story."

"Please tell me Larry doesn't run into anything."

"He doesn't, but the trip he takes us on includes a cliff. We get to it and Lar said over the CB, "On the count of three, we'll gun it and over the ledge we'll go. Like Thelma and Louise. Our tombstones will read: Early Birds flew off in a blaze of glory. Together.""

Betsy didn't know if she wanted to laugh or cry. In an odd way, the scenario made perfect sense. And she'd bet Mary's dream would come to mind when the four of them got in their RVs to leave.

"I know we're wacky enough to consider this, so let me be the first to suggest we find an overhang somewhere."

"Betsy, just so you know, we're not careening to our death. The Lord has more adventures for the Early Birds before our time on earth is done."

"Praise the Lord, Benjamin, and pass the turtle soup."

"My wife has to get her saying in and she better get her hugs in. I looked at the forecast and we're leaving for Florida in the morning."

~~~

"It's time, Bets. You know they're not going to

leave until you tell them goodbye." Ben held his wife's flowered shirt. "Here, put this on."

"The longer I stall, the longer they're here." Betsy sniffled and it had nothing to do with the cold Mary gave her.

"We're on our own mission, dear, with your books. In less than six months we'll see our friends and you can tell them your tales. Catch up on hugs too. Now let's get outside."

Betsy finished getting dressed and checked the mirror to see if she passed inspection. Didn't want to scare them on their last morning together. She also brushed her teeth. With nothing else to make time stand still, she walked downstairs to their kitchen. "I'm ready."

"After you."

Bets opened the door and Rose stood at the bottom of their steps. "Glad you could make an appearance."

"I wanted to sleep in, but Ben made me get up."

"You're fibbing, and you know it. You couldn't wait to send your friends on their way." Rose came over and gave Betsy a hug to carry her until they met again. While they held each other, the blubbering began. Mary came over to add to the music coming out of the other two.

"If we don't separate them, they'll be here until the leaves turn this fall."

"Larry, I'm partial to both of my arms. Any of those three have the ability to chew one of them off."

"I'll go get my wife. You two need to hit the road. As sad as it is to say." Ben hugged his friends then grasped Betsy's hand and led her away. "Come on, hon."

They stood and Bets took off on their theme song. *On the Road Again.*

"Benjamin, while she's signing books, sign her up for music lessons. Our ears will thank us." Rose snorted.

"Until we, or whatever we're calling ourselves, meet again."

"Betsy, you just reminded me. I think our new name should be: Who Are the Birds Blessing Today?"

"You almost have it, Rosie. Lose a few words and we'll call ourselves the Blessing Birds since we go around blessing others."

"Bingo. I love it."

"And with that, the Blessing Birds have taken flight. We'll be in touch."

THE END

Don't miss these other fun novels by Janetta Fudge-Messmer

Early Birds
Southbound Birds
Girly Birds

Salvation Message:

My prayer while writing the Early Birds series was for my readers to come away knowing that the Lord Jesus loves them and prayer works. If you've finished reading and have never asked Jesus Christ into your heart, I'd like to give you the opportunity to do so today.

Lord Jesus, I'm a sinner and I repent of my sins. Please forgive me. I believe Jesus died for my sins and rose again on the third day. Please come into my heart and fill me with Your Holy Spirit. AMEN!

If you prayed this prayer, you probably have questions about what's next:
1) Find a good church that teaches the Bible.
2) Set aside time each day to focus on God by reading your Bible and praying.
3) Develop relationships with people. Try to find a friend in the church you attend who can help you spiritually.
4) Publicly proclaim your new faith in Christ and your commitment to follow Him by being baptized.
5) Check out this website: www.gotquestions.org. They are there to help you out.

Bio:

Janetta Fudge Messmer is an inspirational author, speaker and editor. Her Early Birds series (Early Birds, Southbound Birds, Girly Birds and Blessing Bird) are sure to make you laugh out loud. They may also make you want to hit the road in your own RV. Janetta, her hubby (Ray), and their pooch (Maggie) are full-time RVers. Writing and traveling go hand in hand as they see the USA in their twenty-five foot Minnie Winnie.

LINKS:

Available on Amazon: https://goo.gl/rd0X4T
E-mail: janettafudgemessmer@gmail.com
Website: http://janettafudgemessmer.com/
Blog: http://www.nettie-fudges-world.blogspot.com/
Facebook:
https://www.facebook.com/janetta.fudge.messmer
Twitter: https://twitter.com/nettiefudge